MW01178822

WITHDRAWN

Café des Westens

A Novel

Norman Ravvin

Red Deer College Press

The Publishers
Red Deer College Press
56 Avenue & 32 Street Box 5005
Red Deer Alberta Canada T4N 5H5

Credits
Cover Art by Rick Sealock
Jacket Design by Jim Brennan
Text Design by Dennis Johnson
Typesetting by Boldface Technologies Inc.
Printed & bound in Canada by Gagné Printing Ltée.
for Red Deer College Press

Acknowledgments
The extract from *Lost Berlin* is reprinted by permission of
Bison Books. Copyright © 1979 by Susanne Everett.
The Publishers gratefully acknowledge the financial assistance
of the Canada Council, the Alberta Foundation for the Arts,
Alberta Culture & Multiculturalism, Red Deer College and
Radio 7 CKRD.
The author gratefully acknowledges the assistance of the
Ontario Arts Council.

Canadian Cataloguing in Publication Data
Ravvin, Norman, 1963-
Café des Westens
ISBN 0-88995-079-2
I. Title.
PS8585.A98C3 1991 C813'.54 C91-091300-5
PR9199.3.R38C3 1991

To my mother,
who showed me where to look,

&

To Shelley,
my best friend

Now in midsummer come and all fools slaughtered
And spring's infuriations over and a long way
To the first autumnal inhalations, young broods
Are in the grass, the roses are heavy with a weight
Of fragrance and the mind lays by its trouble.

Now the mind lays by its trouble and considers.
The fidgets of remembrance come to this.
This is the last day of a certain year
Beyond which there is nothing left of time.
It comes to this and the imagination's life.

Wallace Stevens

One

At the Café des Westens

The air had lost its fragrance in the neighborhood of the Café des Westens. No longer was there the rich beery smell of flour being bleached. The Robin Hood Mill, denounced as an eyesore years before, had been torn down with every other structure built before 1960. With the mill went the stockyards, so the wind no longer carried the sharp smell of thawing spring earth, which had blown from the east through all the city's early seasons. Gone as well was the smell of oil from the streetcar tracks. They had been torn up and sold to other cities. Pawned off like cheap ambassadors. These smells had all disappeared, and the summer heat seemed the less for it—there were never enough blossoms in a prairie town to sweeten the breeze. Now, only the rough smell of poplar gum, the scent of caragana seeds wasting in the sun.

The Café des Westens sat beside unleased property, boarded-up property, abandoned property, its old booths and tables like lookouts on the boom-and-bust town. The café remained unchanged, thanks to no effort of its owner or its clientele, while the rest of the city came down and went up around it. The office towers shivered ever so slightly in the prairie wind, hotels and restaurants were remodelled semiannually, one-way streets turned one way and then the other, trees were planted where none had been and uprooted where they had grown. The Café des Westens stood by, even without the fragrance of past years, without the beery smell of bleached flour packed hard into cement silos, without the broad swirling stench of meat and manure.

The café became famous by default. By making no amends to fashion, it stayed well ahead of it. The children of regulars began to bring their friends in. Magazines clamored to photograph its threadbare interior and editorialize on its staying power. When the takers of photographs, the writers of advertorials appeared with their state-of-the-art equipment, they found the place as it had always been. Or so they thought. Martin on the phone as usual. The rest of the café lizards slouched in their chairs, smoking and drinking, chins tipped up to look over the bar at Ostrovsky, who mixed their next round.

Interviewers came by the dozens one summer, when the city was in a particularly festive self-promotional mood, and its commentators were searching everywhere for its mythical heart. At first Ostrovsky appreciated the publicity the media gave him, and he served his visitors the most elaborate sandwiches, the richest coffee and cheesecake they had ever tasted, compliments of the house.

But as these visits grew in number, each reporter with his inevitable collection of cameras and tape recorders began to resemble one generic and completely predictable figure that Ostrovsky remembered only as the Interviewer. And the Interviewer kept returning, kept getting out of his little Triumph or Fiat or whatever it was he drove, his camera and tote bags slung randily over one shoulder.

The Interviewer never tired of standing back on the curb and taking a good look at the café, as if that told him all he needed to know about his subject. And in he came, raising his sunglasses in recognition of Ostrovsky as if he knew too, beyond a doubt, that this was the man he had an appointment with.

Why was the Interviewer never a woman? Ostrovsky wondered. Or an older journalist with Scotch on his breath and his pants loose in the seat? And why could he not develop a different approach? Just once. He might choose a different booth to dump his belongings in. Not the most desirable one by the front window. He might be more inconspicuous with the muzzle of his camera, less feverish with the flash. The Interviewer went from corner to corner, testing his light source, sending the white bursts streaking up the walls like staged lightning. He took pictures of the bar and the line of booths that overlooked the avenue, and shots of the red glow thrown by the exit sign near the washrooms. He photographed the arc of white lettering painted on the window that read CAFÉ DES WESTENS, the soft blue violet of evening hanging behind it. And he photographed Ostrovsky over and over as he crossed the room, stopping at each table to make sure his customers were satisfied, and then once for good measure as Ostrovsky extended his right hand and raised the left to shield his eyes.

Ostrovsky offered the Interviewer a drink, but the offer was always declined. A professional, the Interviewer preferred to get right down to work. He started his tape recorder whirring and settled down with his list of questions and wise remarks, the first of which was always the same.

—Your café is becoming a landmark, Mr. Ostrovsky.

Sometimes the Interviewer was quite formal, and at other times he casually assumed first-name basis with his subject.

—Have you got any idea why it's such a success?

Ostrovsky found the whirring center of the Interviewer's machine hypnotizing. It made him want to tell lies.

—I've got a good location.

—But it could be better, surely. You're a little far east for the downtown crowds, and there's nothing nearby that does business after six. A couple of gas stations and a little variety store.

—It used to be a busier neighborhood.

—But what's bringing the younger people out?

—I don't really know. Things come and go.

—What about the name? It's a catchy one.

—I chose it because it's hard to pronounce.

Ostrovsky sneaked a quick look around the café.

—But you must have had something in mind when you chose it.

—The name means less than you think.

—How do you mean that?

—Well, at first I called it nothing.

—The Café Nothing?

—No, just nothing. That struck me as somehow appropriate in a city where the streets all have numbers instead of names. But that's not entirely true. Some streets in Calgary have Indian names. But I wasn't about to name my restaurant after Crazy Horse. That kind of thing wasn't in style when I was starting out. Imagine, the Crazy Horse Café.

—I think there's one in Winnipeg.

—But not in Calgary.

—No, I guess not.

—Chief Big Bear Café. Chief Chinikee Cocktail Bar. That sort of thing would have sent me hurtling toward bankruptcy.

—A name means that much?

—Sure. People like to feel comfortable. No one would have come in. Maybe a few drifters looking for the adventure they were too tired to look for on the road. Otherwise, nobody wants to be reminded. Know what I mean?

—No, I'm not sure. . . .

—Well, you tell me. What do you see when you look west to the foothills? All that prairie fenced and neatly trimmed. Roads rising on big humped hills. Ranch homes with satellite dishes out back. It's easy to believe there was nothing there before all this.

—Nothing?

—Nothing. See what I mean? The Crazy Horse Café. It's nothing. Says nothing. Believe me, I know. Nobody eats where the place reminds them of nothing. People want to eat where they're reminded of something big. Sailing ships! The Vimy Ridge! Sir John A. Macdonald!

—Big names.

—Right. No small-timers or losers. But at first I thought I'd do things differently. I didn't like any of the names that came to mind. The Grill. Hy's Place. You know, names you could get off any television show. So I called it nothing. I just opened up. But no one came in. I mean no one. Not even drifters. People would come up to the window and look in, back up, stand with their hands in their pockets looking up for a sign. They checked the door for proof that this really was a restaurant. All the time I was behind the bar with my apron on. The tables were set, and the stove top was obviously waiting for me to slap the first eggs down and push 'em around in the grease. You know what I mean?

—Well, go on.

—Everybody thought it was a front. No name, no sign. Gotta be a front. Now a front is interesting. Everybody wants to know what's being fronted. But no one dared to sit and see what I'd serve up in my nameless front for untold dirty doings.

—So what did you do?

—I tried a few temporary names. I just wrote them on a chalkboard that I stood up in the window. I was still intent on not going back to the old standbys.

—Mm hm.

—So I tried Mimi's. I thought that sounded friendly but still sort of enigmatic. Cute. As if the place had a fairy godmother overseeing things. But when people saw me serving the eggs, they felt cheated. Every plate I served, you name it, down to the last steak sandwich, these people were peeking around behind my back, trying to see who was in the kitchen. They were hoping to find a jolly fat Italian woman serving ice cream. Someone who'd cross her fingers and shout *Malokia!* if you talked dirty.

—Mimi would have reminded them of something?

—Absolutely. A taste of Italy. The canals. The Pope. Other good things. It's not much, but it's better than nothing.

—And the name you chose?

—Well, it came to me very much by chance. I've been told since that it's a very suggestive name to those in the know. And I suppose that's fine, if you have a taste for nostalgia, which I don't. I didn't intend to conjure up any ghosts. When I decided to put some signage out front, I wanted to know what the standard piece of neon cost. There was a character who had a sign shop over on Seventeenth Avenue. I think he was a cousin of Menachem Begin's. He'd done something shifty with diamonds during the war. He took me into his storeroom at the back of his shop to give me an idea of what things cost. The first sign he showed me is what's been out front of the café for the past thirty years. He'd bought it as part of a junk lot that came by train from Montreal. Where it came from before that, nobody knows. He paid fifty bucks for a truckload of chairs and stained glass, coat racks, old photographs of French singers. A ton of books. Real junk. Plus the sign. He plugged it into six other things to make it work. He had a snake of lamps and extension cords patched up and plugged into the wall somewhere. I figured he was running quite a fire hazard and told him I could do without the demonstration. But he'd gotten very busy getting it all set up, and I think he might have forgotten I was there as he burrowed around looking for live wires. When the thing came on I pretty near had a heart attack.

—Impressive?

—Just bright. Bang! I was sure the fuses in his place would blow.

—So you bought it?

—I had to. It was a very good buy.

—I like the way the neon birds flap their wings.

—Those are my swallows.

—Swallows?

—I think they're swallows. They're so sleek and white. I thought it would be nice to have those swallows flying above my new place. For luck.

The Interviewer always lost interest at this point, just as Ostrovsky was about to introduce the air and the way it smelled before the mill was torn down, before the streetcar tracks were packed off as scrap. The Interviewer had expert instincts, could smell the rise of irrelevant detail and color a mile off. Ostrovsky never got to talk about his father or the old-timers who made his place their second home. He was cut off the moment his voice betrayed even a hint of nostalgia.

Some distraction, like the racket of milk shakes being shaken, presented the Interviewer with an insurmountable technical challenge. His sound meters flapping, he suggested he had enough material.

Ostrovsky agreed and asked the young man whether he wouldn't rather be doing something else on such a pretty evening. The summer air was tempting, twilit and scented beyond the café's big front window. Certainly the night had a personality worth engaging, worth looking into. It was just a tougher interview than some. There was the fine trelliswork of shadow that trees traced between themselves. The shapes of cars, exaggerated beasts by the sidewalk. And the air, gathered into bodies of heat, breeze and dankness, with pockets of cool behind lilac bushes one could search out. It was as if the summer evening knew how to gather itself, how to take up poses.

Ostrovsky was glad to show the Interviewer the door. He stood on the step to be polite, watched the man amble up the street, unlock his car and set the tape recorder on the roof as he opened the door. Then he got in, started his smart little engine and drove away with the black box perched and ready to take flight.

Inside, Ostrovsky noticed anxious faces scanning the café in search of service. Martin was still in the phone booth getting mileage out of his quarter.

Regulars

"Yes. Haven't I told you twice already that I will? Hmm? No. I won't forget. If I forget I'll be hearing about it next year. Repeat it? Mother, you're going to make me mad. Oh. Two pounds of flour instead of five? Sure. And five pounds of potatoes. Which type of yogurt? Strawberry. If they have it. And an egg loaf, sliced. Yes, I wrote it all down." Holding the receiver between his shoulder and cheek, patting his shirt and pants pockets for a pen, Martin listens to the familiar requests. He flips through the yellow pages in search of a blank space to use as note paper, but the shopping list goes unremembered for the second time.

His mother shifts into a long story about the plumber and a cat. Martin half-listens, more or less following her rhythm so he can answer her with the right expressions of agreement. Across the café a waiter serves a tray of drinks to a fivesome who look like Sunday drinkers, the kind who order a round only because it is embarrassing not to want a drink. They would probably prefer to put the three dollar expense toward a new pair of socks. If they were to go to the track, they also would be Sunday bettors—people who win by putting money down on the horse with the nicest leg warmers. It is Martin's firm belief that people like this waste luck and liquor.

There is a trick to listening to his mother's anecdotes. He answers yes to everything, evading the questions he doesn't hear by clearing his throat or interrupting her, as if he is in the kitchen cooking something and must keep checking to see if it's burning. Seeing such a lot of drink going to people who don't appreciate it makes him heartsick. Just as the changing clientele in the Café des Westens makes him heartsick. Besides the clientele, nothing else in the place has changed. Martin grew up with the man who owns the café, Hiram Ostrovsky, chief cook and bottle washer—and resident ironist—who chose the ridiculously European name for the business he opened in this most Canadian of towns. With the resolve of a man whose stubbornness verges on fanaticism, Ostrovsky has kept the name on the old neon sign in place long enough for such names and neon signs to go in and out of style at least three times. Suddenly the name and the sign are very much in fashion again. As are the café's Naugahyde swivel stools and the shelves lined with jars of gray pickled eggs. The drinks have always been in demand, served in plastic water glasses, badly mixed, rarely tasting the way their names suggest they should. Ostrovsky is always saying, "You don't have to give 'em what's good, Martin. They don't know what's good."

This philosophy seems to pay off. There is always a big rush at last call, a flurry of ordering among the art student and welfare crowd who gather drinks as insurance that they won't be kicked out for at least a half-hour. Ostrovsky doesn't seem to mind the trendy set that has taken over his restaurant. He keeps up, the way he always has, with the latest news from Israel and the stock reports. And he stands drinks for the fat retired bus driver who sits at the bar and sings the choruses from Gaelic folk songs in a throaty tenor.

Martin is attached to the eggs and the phlegmy folk songs. But he can't adapt to the temper of semibohemia that has settled over the café. Once he's sung his old refrain—Good-night, mother, I'll call you tomorrow, good-night, have a good sleep—he wishes he could push the whole crowd, except the tenor by the eggs and one or two others, into the hot wind and watch them stand, bewildered, skirts flapping, hair down in their eyes. Then he would order them to disperse, vanish, evaporate, to lean west and keep on leaning till they fell over.

Ostrovsky is doubled, reflected in the big mirror behind the bar, his belly waving at itself as he shakes martini mix in a silver-plated jug. Martin winds up the bar toy that sits by the till, a bug-eyed red-jacketed bartender that whirs and clicks as its arms mimic Ostrovsky's. The real bartender sets his jug of liquor down, picks up his imitator and drops it in a drawer.

"How's your mother, Martin?"

"She's fine. As good as can be expected. But her two boarders are driving her crazy."

"I tell you, she should get out of that house. It's too much for her. My dad, when I put him in the lodge last year, it was the best thing that could have happened to him."

"She's tough, Hy. She still thinks she's a young woman."

Ostrovsky divides what is in the martini shaker into two stubby glasses, which look as though they might have been gifts at a gas station. He keeps the glass with the picture of the Rockies for himself and slides the one with the Calgary Tower across the countertop.

"Is she still trying to fix you up?"

Martin shrugs, turns the Calgary Tower toward the mirror. "She's given that one a rest lately. It's Max she's worried about. She thinks he's going to get himself in trouble because he hangs out with a bunch of musicians and filmmakers. She's sure they're all dope dealers. Corrupters of her innocent grandson."

"She's sentimental, Martin. That comes from growing up in a place where there was at least the belief in something better. And to her a twenty-two year old is still a baby. But how is Max? I haven't seen him since he started driving cab."

"I don't see him much. He wants to move out. He says he's tired of me reaching into my pocket for him, and he wants a place where he can invite his friends over. He's always up to something with his girlfriend and his buddies."

"Well, at least he's got friends." Ostrovsky eyes a sloppy-looking drunk sliding slowly but steadily off his chair. This is a member of the old contingent of men who get drunk sullenly, silently, without any fanfare or fancy conversation. Beyond the window the empty street is an odd emerald color in the lamplight, the window of a drug and soda shop brightening and then disappearing beneath a yellow neon strip. Surveying this empire, Martin realizes Ostrovsky is not the best person to study family matters with—an old bachelor, his head in his ledger books, his new-found popularity making him rich in his late middle age. Still, it's embarrassing to admit that your kid would rather do without you, and Martin wishes his old friend would offer some guidance. Ostrovsky firms up the sliding drunk, pulls his elbows together so they will hold him up and disappears behind the swinging doors leading to the back room. With no one left to confide in, Martin watches the drunk in the mirror. The man's eyes are half-closed, his fingers slipping into his nose as he begins again to slide off his seat.

Martin wonders when it was that Max and he began to grow apart. Certainly he can remember the first time he felt he'd let his son down. It was just before Max's mother died. Max was six or seven, and Martin had taken him to a birthday party. When he picked him up, Martin suggested they go downtown to look at the bleachers being set up for the weekend parade. He'd brought his old Instamatic along and tried to make Max feel important, the way Martin remembered feeling when his parents took him to have his portrait taken.

The bleachers rose and spread like the skeleton of an unfinished tower. Max peered into the complicated shadows underneath the metal rails and broad wooden seats, then sat himself down on the lowest plank, looking very sad in the costume he'd worn to his friend's party. His feet were swimming in a pair of his father's dress shoes, which were strapped on like old-fashioned roller skates, the laces wrapped under the instep and over the top of the shoes to keep them from flapping. He wore an old-fashioned suit coat, with the sleeves held above his wrists by two elastics off the morning mail. The jacket was buttoned so he nearly disappeared inside it, and on his head was Martin's thin-brimmed wedding hat, a gray Stetson Max could have just as easily curled up in as worn. He looked like a sad circus clown, with his chin jutting from under the hat, the lapels of his jacket tickling his ears.

Martin stood back with the camera and clicked away. When the roll of film was finished, he stayed put on the sidewalk and watched his son, who seemed to be trying to disappear inside his costume.

Martin had no idea what a child should know about death. If Max asked about heaven, what could he have said? That he had no strong feelings about it either way? It was terrible that Max had waited so anxiously for his mother to get out of the hospital, never even knowing why she was there, hopeful that once it was done everything would be back to the way it should be. They thought they had caught the cancer. And though Max's mother was sent home, the shock of what had happened was too much. Some silent reevaluation had gone on in the operation's aftermath, and she came home silent and exhausted. She did nothing but sit under a blanket on the back patio, watching the waves of wind rush through the trees at the edge of the yard.

Martin took Max to see the parade route to keep him out of the house. It was late enough in the afternoon that there wasn't much traffic, and Martin parked near the row of bleachers that snaked around the lot behind his funeral home. Standing on the topmost bench he could see how the tar on the roof was holding up.

"Tomorrow we'll come to see the Indians and cowboys. And the mayor."

Max sank deeper into the camouflage of his Stetson and his upturned collar.

"How about that, Max? Indians."

Max tipped his hat up on his forehead so he could meet Martin's eyes, but the brim slipped down again. From under the Stetson he asked, "Indians?"

The white tabletops flash as a car pulls a U-turn outside the café. Coats hung on wall hooks seem to signal to one another in the shifting shadow. A bowl of fruit on the window ledge glows a brilliant red, then withers.

Max's girlfriend has joined the group that ordered the tray of drinks, and she stands with her hands on the back of an empty chair, apparently trying to convince the others to leave. Sara waves, interrupting the scornful stare Martin has been directing at all the half-empty glasses. For some reason, looking at Sara always makes Martin sad, in the same way a very quiet sweet piece of music makes him imagine melancholy fantasies. She is blessed with the kind of Mediterranean beauty that makes white skin seem less than worthy. A wonderful Semitic face full of clouds and darkening years. But hers is not an approachable beauty, as far as he can tell. There is something asexual about it, holy, even ghostlike. Martin last saw Sara a month ago, when she and Max insisted on spending the evening with him. The three of them sat in the front room of his apartment with their hands in their laps, and Martin shooed them out early, though he didn't want them to leave, because he was sure they were performing a charitable act.

Martin would like to go over to her, single her out from her friends and find out how she's been, but Ostrovsky is on top of them like a herdsman, poking and sweet-talking his patrons into going home. Sara and her companions pull on their jackets. One woman puts a black felt hat with a broken crown on her head. All five dig into their pockets to make up the tip. They are squeezed down the entranceway and out onto the street before Martin can make a move.

Ostrovsky takes the wind-up barkeep out of the drawer, turns the key in its backside and sets it on the bar. Martin watches the little man rock on his motorized rubber arms. Years ago he might have asked Ostrovsky if he could have the doll as a present for Max. Now when he leaves, he leaves empty-handed, hurrying into the familiar street to join the rest of the home-bound crowd.

The old-timers make their slow way up the avenue, keeping close to the squat old buildings. The younger crowd makes a game out of zigzagging around the skeletal trees, weaving out into the street and back onto the sidewalk. Sara is nowhere in sight. The ever-present profile appears in the house across the street, a woman, reading a palm-sized book by the light of a lamp perched on her mantle.

At the Funeral Home

The police know Martin well. They know his car, a black late-model Lincoln sedan, and the times it is likely to be found in the parking lot of his funeral home with him inside, asleep, too drunk to even consider driving. One of the car's features is its spacious front seat where Martin can lie down comfortably.

There are times when Martin sleeps in the car on purpose to avoid his apartment. His rooms play tricks on him when he is drunk. They change their shape and rearrange their layout. Doors move a foot or two to the right of where they are supposed to be. The legs of chairs spread like splayed tentacles across the floor. And as if it isn't enough that architecture and furnishings conspire against him, his coordination and reflexes become hopeless. His ankles turn on the slightest ripple in the rug. His hands never come out of his pockets fast enough to prevent his face from smashing into the floor. And his apartment block is a breeding ground for gossips and pathological voyeurs, people who have lived in the same place so long they feel it is their right to know the condition of their neighbors when they arrive home at odd hours. The building's eccentric design invites this surveillance. Each apartment has a window that provides a view of the common hallway from the kitchen, an unnecessary and unorthodox view, but one the tenants are very attached to. Almost no one tires of the opportunity to watch the traffic of familiar faces and strangers going up and down the hall. It is impossible to come home dishevelled, on an unfamiliar arm, and not be watched by a closet detective pretending to hang curtains.

Gossips with subtler methods lurk to the side of their kitchen window, using their apartment—a Vermeer-like tangle of doors and passageways—to catch the attention of passersby. Stopping, watching, the unknowing snoops become the victims of their own curiosity.

Martin can never resist a quick look into his neighbor's kitchen. It is stocked with hundreds of jars full of spice and cooking mysteries. An elaborate set of ceramic pots hangs on nails like art pieces above a round table with wrought iron legs. The cupboards and countertops are painted in glossy reds and greens. Once Martin saw the apartment's two tenants cooking together. One man stood in front of the stove stirring and ladling, while the other clasped his partner from behind. Martin guessed the second man might affect the outcome of the recipe by how hard he squeezed, each squeeze a signal to the cook that too much of this had been added, not enough of that.

On every trip he made down the hallway, no matter how respectable he looked and acted, Martin felt eyes on him. He watched carefully for the telltale orange glow of a cigarette by the window casement.

Sometimes Martin fell asleep in his car without meaning to, with the radio on, buzzing and rattling as stations bled into one another, the rumble of some manic virtuoso bashing out a newly discovered bit of Wagner rising above and then disappearing beneath the croon of the latest Frank Sinatra sound-alike.

Martin woke before dawn on these mornings to the click of his ignition key, a crisply ironed coat sleeve under his nose. An amused face, mustachioed and topped with a cap, said, "Morning, Mr. Binder," or, "Didn't want you to burn out your battery." Following which Martin always felt an overwhelming jolt of fear that the officer might ask him to breathe into a bag or order him to walk on a line chalked so lightly on the pavement that it looked like the soft edge of a shadow. But this never happened. Martin began to feel he had special privileges for sleeping in cars drunk, walking the streets drunk, listening to loud radio music drunk, as long as he didn't try to drive the big Lincoln drunk. After a night's sleep in the car he was usually sober, but if he felt the slightest bit listless he locked the car and walked home, tracing imaginary chalk lines far ahead of him on the sidewalk. If he'd had a bag he would have breathed into it, filling it with rejuvenated if somewhat stale breath, and carried the package home like a child's balloon, a prize won at a carnival.

A Matter of Estrangement

Martin did not have to live alone. That is, he had the choice between his quiet conspiratorial apartment, where his son made unpredictable appearances and disappearances, and his old bedroom in his mother's house on Twelfth Avenue. That is where he belonged since he became a widower—according to the responsibilities of kin and common humanity—in the house where his mother sat alone, day after day, peeling an orange in the afternoon, taking a cup of tea in the evening. Holding tightly on to the handrail as she made her way up and down stairs, dragging her laundry or a damp mop for dusting. It didn't matter how much he visited. She still complained he was too far away, too hard to reach. And she seemed to have an endless catalogue of friends who fell down stairs, were assaulted by paperboys and plumbers, took the wrong medicine at the wrong time of day and wound up in hospital. Who were all these people who plummeted down stairwells? Did they do these things to spite him?

Martin had no intention of moving home. It was ridiculous for his mother to expect him to. What would he do in his old room?

Search the drawers for envelopes he'd left behind. Read his old love letters, which smelled now like mothballs and pine. Try on the electric orange and emerald green silk ties hung neatly in the closet on a plastic tie rack. Peek in the little crawlspace beside his room, an unfinished corner under one end of the roof beams, now a museum of items too old to be of any use but too curious to throw away: desk lamps with webbed iron feet and dried-out rotten cords, unstrung tennis rackets with gut so brittle it snapped like spaghetti, briefcases packed full of bills, letters, schoolwork, clippings, pages torn from books.

The bedroom was unlivable. The walls were painted hospital green and decorated with unrecognizable landscapes in plastic frames. Even the design on the linoleum was strange, swirling and hypnotic like a child's scribbling. Martin had only bad memories of the years when the room was his domain, with his mother yelling at him through the closed door and the sickening smell of cabbage and chicken—both boiled—wafting up through the radiator. Surely this was a torture he'd dreamed of and not one he'd experienced. Why would his mother want to reenact even a part of it? It was better to peel an orange in peace. To take a cup of tea with a cookie, watch the news and go to bed.

But emotional blackmail was a popular tactic in Martin's family. He could not remember his father using it, but his mother was an expert, and by some dreadful irony she had passed none of her skill on to her son, who was helpless before it. She had even taken on the orphaned daughter of distant relatives as a kind of cause célèbre—the girl's parents had been killed in a spectacular fire in the early fifties when the poultry warehouse that had stood beside their home, stolid and stinking for decades, exploded in some freak spontaneous combustion brought on by too much overheated sawdust. The child was out at a piano lesson as the block burned, and when she returned, the air was thick with yellow haze and the unmistakable aroma of roasted chicken. Martin's mother took Edith in after the accident, and the girl lived in her adopted home until the late sixties when she followed the prevalent trend and enacted a kind of rebellion, evicting the tenants of a house her parents had owned before they were killed and moving in herself.

Edith had been on her own for more than twenty years, but Martin's mother continued to treat her like the helpless victim of an ongoing tragedy. She talked to Martin at length about Edith's visits and described the rare favor she did at length, as if to insinuate that besides this daughter of another woman she had no real family of her own.

Martin and Edith were his mother's last contact with a large family, which had died off around her, providing her son with the only kind of business he didn't want. The rest were left behind, shadows on the ground in other lands. And this was a loss that could not be made up for, not even by the most attentive son. Martin understood that his mother's obsession with Edith was enacted as some kind of compensation for her loss. She had convinced him to give Edith a job in his funeral parlor. His mother even enlisted him as helpmate, delivering groceries and carefully boxed cakes that she struggled over—hard labor it was on a hot summer day—insisting they must arrive at Edith's house still warm out of the oven. His mother had a key cut so he could leave his gifts inside should Edith not be at home.

But Edith knew she had Mrs. Binder where she wanted her. She was an emotional blackmailer par excellence herself, and based on this family resemblance, it occurred to Martin that he might be the orphaned foundling and Edith the legitimate only child. She had developed a repertoire of manipulative maneuvers: she would leave her phone off the hook for a week, giving the impression of foul play, and then appear at dinner time, dishevelled, with an eye on what was broiling, a quick peak beneath the top of the soup pot. She even sent the odd marble cake back with the explanation that she was on a diet.

Edith treated Martin with the same cocky aplomb. When he arrived at her door bearing a pair of nylons and a carton of Players

—courtesy of his mother—she would hint that the cigarettes were stale, complain about the brand of the nylons and then manage to suggest they were brought more in the name of a guilt offering than goodwill. She even once called Martin's mother a busybody, as he stood, a marble cake warming his shirt front. Martin abandoned his usual conciliatory manner, shouting, "She's been a good friend to you, for God's sake," and pushed the box at Edith, backing out of her stale front hall, which smelled of cooking grease, perfume and cigarettes.

Following this incident, Martin gave up. He accepted that his mother was addicted to indulging Edith's perverse whims. He would have to face the disturbances and leave things as they were.

Martin took his mother shopping. He sent plumbers over when the pipes knocked. Sometimes he sent his friends to her house to take care of repairs. They usually did a bad job and gave his mother some new unpleasantness to dwell on. Mackenzie, an unemployed old classmate of Martin's, built a fence around the backyard that fell down in midsummer and squashed a thriving crop of lilies and dahlias. Soon after he built the fence, Mackenzie climbed an immense wooden ladder with a pair of pruners fixed to a stick and tried to trim the crab apple tree. The weight of the ladder, added to the girth of the man, snapped the old tree in half. Mackenzie, the ladder and the top half of the tree went through the roof of a neighbor's garage.

Martin's mother got on the phone and yelled, "This is help? With help like this I'd be better off alone."

"There was a time," she told him later, peeling an orange carefully with a knife, "when we had a man to do these things. To plant a tree or cut the lawn."

"I can't change the way things are, mother."

"That you should want to, though. That's what matters."

"That I should want to what?"

"Change things." She put a piece of orange in her mouth but didn't chew it, holding it instead against the inside of her cheek.

"By that you mean get married, right mother?"

"That wouldn't hurt. You've been a widower now for too long. It makes you act funny, I think. Why don't you look for some-one?"

He looked at her over the arrangement of plastic flowers that stood in an earthenware vase in the center of the table. He watched the bottom of her face move as she worked at squeezing the juice from the piece of orange. There was bone there. More bone than he had ever imagined could hide behind the shape and fullness of a face. And the color in her cheeks, not painted on but rising at the thought of him changing things, was blotchy and showed only in little hollows above her smile. It was as if the exact pores where her blush originated could be traced and counted. Her eyes though, Martin thought, are as they always were. Moist. Expressive. Beautiful things caught and wasting in a desolate place. Upon them formed a cusp, a border between one world— an inner one, beautiful and old under mist and yellow groundsels —and another outer world, made up of nothing but the rush of moments, the birds outside in the grass, the house with its broken tree and fallen fence, the coiled orange rind. All these latter things had to be accepted as the tedious outcome of a long life, the everyday business that was a continuous reminder of what had become of what had been.

But behind the eye, caught in the bowl of flesh and vein, there was a vanished Polish city. A pale of nurturing and calm. There, one need not be concerned with what lay outside a certain circle of safety. One knew how much of the silverware was hidden in the attic and how much black beer was cooling in the cellar, fitted into a hole in the dirt wall. In this place steeples reached not very high, and Polish streets stretched not very wide, with a thin gutter run-ning down their middle, which cast away with the evening rain all that did not belong. Martin's mother looked out at him through these rains, looked out at him from under the shadows that fell from the peaks of buildings lining Plock Street, the *Mlawer Gasse,* the Old Market. She called him by another name in her heart, imagined him wearing different clothes.

Martin lived out among the specks of dust. Under the broken crab apple tree. Tangled up in the smashed lilies. He was *shmutsik.* Dirty. Mrs. Binder's son was a *shmutsiker mensch.*

At the Kitchen Table

Martin wondered if there had ever been such a thing as a Polish boomtown. He pictured an oil well spouting in a peasant's cabbage patch, and bingo, goodbye to the old days. Out with the irrigation equipment and rusty plows, in with the derricks and steel pipe; sharpies from Warsaw show up with leather valises full of junk bonds; the town is overrun by cheap kielbasa stands and saloons where there were once candy shops and polite tea rooms. Martin's mother never spoke about a Polish boom. Her hometown had survived Bolsheviks and Pilsudski, the pleasant streets filled, for a season, with banner-waving recruits putting on an act borrowed from a warped fairy tale.

For Martin, the boom in Calgary began on the Sunday morning in March, more than ten years before, when the Wales Hotel was demolished. He hadn't set foot in the Wales Café in years. When Ostrovsky opened the Café des Westens, Martin had committed his patronage to his friend. But the hotel still bore a weight of familiarity he felt he should honor. Its destruction marked the beginning of the end of the city he'd grown up in.

Headlines on the day following the demolition announced that

"Most Calgarians Slept" as the landmark bit the dust, but Martin marked the event in a less blasé fashion. By sunup he had bought a Saturday *Herald,* driven downtown and parked around the corner from the hotel. He left his car far enough away to make sure it wouldn't be dusted with exploded masonry and perched himself in the alcove of a shuttered jewelry shop across the street from the Wales. He watched the team of men who wore gray overalls— "Cleveland Demolition" emblazoned on their backs—as they dragged boxes of what Martin guessed must be dynamite up the hotel's front steps. This seemed an unnecessary affront. Couldn't the weapons of destruction go in through a service entrance? The Wales was to be the first building in Canada destroyed not by a wrecking ball, the slow and honorable tradition of demolition, but by dynamite. Work that normally would have taken a month would be finished in a matter of minutes.

Once the men had gone inside, Martin went back to his newspaper. *Serpico* was at the Grand. Ostrovsky had told him it was worth seeing. The forecast high for the day was a few degrees above zero. Supreme Court Judge Sirica had ruled that a secret grand jury report investigating Nixon's role in the Watergate scandal should be released to the House. A three-foot-long jawbone, all that was left of a forerunner to the hairy mammoth, had been unearthed near Svetozzrevo, Yugoslavia. Martin was mouthing the name, *Svet–ozz–revo,* trying different pronunciations, when he saw the three Cleveland men exit the Wales' front door, pulling it shut behind them. They crossed the street to a square of pavement marked by four bright orange pylons and began opening a box full of wire and electrical tape. The last thing Martin read was Monday's forecast—clearing, highs to 45—when he heard a sound, like the ripping of a piece of canvas, magnified immensely. He realized this was the prolonged sound of bricks being compressed, crushing one another, as the explosion, muffled in the center of the hotel, brought the building down around it. The Wales was gone almost before he could look up. Overhead, a shred of curtain, blown aloft through an open window, fluttered and turned as it fell to the street.

Over the next few years, exploding buildings caught on the way dances caught on in the old jazz clubs in Harlem. It was happening on every block. People came out to watch. There was the odd casualty as stray pieces of plywood and cinder blocks came rocketing out of nowhere onto pedestrians' heads. But still, you could have sold tickets. The boys from Cleveland Demolition were photographed often, smiling, in front of another successfully pancaked landmark. No conservation groups challenged the carnage. The city was making history—as the wisdom of the day went—so it didn't have to worry about preserving its heritage. As the town boomed and money was made, Martin set aside his sentimental attachment to buildings like the Wales. The city's population grew by tens of thousands each year, and his accountant made a very impressive effort at reporting the funeral home's rising revenue, without adding any snide remarks about the rising death rate that went with the emigration of over-excited fortune-hunting crowds from across the country. People brought their hard luck and illnesses and bad habits with them and, chasing the big time, died under the soft breath of the Chinook.

This was old news. It had been years already since things had begun to slow down, but out of the blue, the land-rush had come one day to Martin's mother's doorstep in the form of Sven-Bjorn Investments, a holding company run by two reclusive brothers who didn't seem to realize real estate prices were faltering in the downtown and had offered an outrageous sum for his mother's little house.

Martin's mother treated the brothers' offer like the arrival of a plague. These speculators were, to her, modern day Bolsheviks, Pilsudskis who'd mistaken the Bow River for the Don. Like all ideologues, they made use of slogans and vague promises to entice people into giving up their ordinary lives.

Sven and Bjorn hired a pair of agents who lurked in the shrubbery, waiting for Martin or his mother to open the front door, so they could launch a new pitch: Bjorn and Sven were looking for one last Canadian property; Sven and Bjorn would only be able to maintain their offer for another week; Sven and Bjorn were liquid now, but a new capital tax was going to tie them up for the rest of the century, and then where would poor Mrs. Binder be?

Martin's mother wouldn't consider a move. A house was not something you traded like an old pair of shoes. A house ensured an ordered customary day. But beyond this, Martin realized that his mother was scared. Friends of hers had sold their houses, auctioned dining and living room sets, gathered their clothes into plastic bags and moved to new apartments, where they died. The money meant nothing to her—her son took care of himself, Edith had a trust fund and she herself had no use for a windfall.

When Martin came over for a cup of tea, he would ask about the agents—whether they'd been by lately, if they had phoned, soft-voiced at dinner time, with an improved offer. Martin's mother threw the collection of business cards the agents left her into a drawer beside the fridge where they became tangled with loose bits of twine, rusty scissors and the fabulous sheets of cake recipes —a scramble of measurements and Yiddish script.

Martin's pitch in favor of selling the house was not inspired by any ulterior motive. He thought his mother might enjoy the company in an old folks home, the activities, a community.

She had nothing to say to these suggestions. The community Martin described was of a modern variety—he realized, as he struggled to pay lip service to his plan—where strangers played cards and gathered on Sunday afternoons to dance along with an out-of-tune piano. He realized what a sham this was. And yet he still thought it was a better use of time than his mother's ritual ceiling washing, toaster shining, her wringing of summer dust from kitchen curtains. He was reminded again and again, as they discussed the changing neighborhood, of the gulf that existed between them in their expectations, their idea of the good life.

This distance made a puzzle of daily life. He never knew what should remain unsaid, what he was supposed to say. And each bit of knowledge had to be approached by stealth. Only easy questions could be asked outright. An easy question involved particulars, such as the three smooth chestnuts Martin picked up in front of the building where he lived.

"They're nice, aren't they, mother?" Martin pushed one nearer to her teacup. His mother agreed and was quiet. Then she asked what they were.

Martin laughed. He knew she wasn't trying to be funny, but there was something outrageous and joyful about her innocence.

"It's like a nut. They grow in the trees on the street where I live." He put his hands in the air to signify busy growth. "Squirrels eat them." Still the picture would not come clear. His impression of a tree only confused things. His mother put the chestnut down as if it suddenly occurred to her it might be dirty.

"What's a squirrel?"

Martin wasn't certain if the word was unfamiliar or if his mother had really never seen a squirrel. He described a long thin animal with a bushy tail that clings to branches.

His mother nodded. "Like a cat."

The woman who rented a room upstairs in the house had befriended an alley cat that sat in trees. It never leapt from a perch once it had settled, but there was still something menacing and disgusting about all that mangy fur and agile muscle hanging above ground ready to pounce on passersby.

"Not really, mother. A squirrel is wild. You don't keep it as a pet." Martin's mother made no sign that she recognized the difference between a squirrel and a cat. She had a different conception than he of what was tame and suitable for bringing into the house. Disagreement over such things defined the distance between them. They rarely agreed about what was trustworthy and what was a threat. What was meaningful and what was simply wildness.

Martin remembered his first boyhood realization that the world was, for him, something to be lived in differently, grasped at and gathered more heartily than it was for his mother. His family, with all its not-yet-dead-yet-distant members, had driven to Banff. The day began very blue and calm, but by early afternoon fat dark thunderclouds were roaming the sky, the color of slate at their peaks, dwindling to a softer more dispersed gray near the bottom. Bits of blue and the fuzzy triangles of distant rainfall warned of an approaching storm. The storm burst, scattering leaves and cooling the hot day with its moist wind when Martin, his uncles and little cousins were busy claiming the swimming pool as their own. The pool deck cleared as the rain blew horizontally across the water on the wind. Even the most obnoxious showman of a child could find no fun in this.

The storm was muffled inside the pool's changing rooms. Martin appeared in the vestibule of the pool's lobby, half-dressed and wet, to listen for more thunder and to count the seconds between the sound of clouds crashing and the flash of lightning. Or did lightning come before the thunderclap? He wasn't sure and decided to get himself outside in the rain to watch for evidence.

Another child stood by a bench, his wet hair sticking up on his head. He looked over the guardrail, down at the pool, and his aloneness, his intrepid peeking, made Martin think of his mother, who would have pulled him back from the untrustworthy railing. He looked through the window at the boy and back at the crowd in the pool lobby to see if he was being watched.

The rain came down on the wind in long gray sheets. The boy looked vulnerable, as if the storm might sweep him away. His bare knees were pressed against the low railing. But he also seemed to belong there—small and still. His concentration was perfect, as if the hot pool, steaming now in the mountain rain, fixed apparitions only he could see. And though he was just another boy in shorts with a bad haircut, he was a spellbound boy, and Martin felt drawn to him. He imagined he must be some kind of hero.

Martin's mother was busy brushing out his cousin's hair. She counted each stroke and finished the fiftieth with a flourish, pushing on toward a hundred. Martin put his towel over his head, half as a canopy and half as camouflage, and went out in the storm, rain rushing down his neck and the backs of his legs.

He crossed the walkway and stood with his hero for a moment. Neither acknowledged the other, their twenty little toes pointing out over the blue pool at Mount Rundle and the headwaters of the Bow River. A few premature fall leaves, brown and curling, circled and dropped into the pool. Martin lowered his towel a bit (a gentleman taking off his coat to invite conversation). He eyed his partner in the rain who did not turn, looked at the boy's roughened knuckles, his long light eyelashes. He thought of solemn promises, duels to the death that only they, bravers of the storm, could take part in.

But none of this would come to be. Their comradeship was cut short as Martin felt a hand around his wrist, a tug at his soaked towel that wrenched it from his grip. His mother pulled him by the arm back across the flagstones to the pool lobby. She sat him down like a doll on a bench and told him to stay put.

He might have fallen! There was lightning in the clouds! Didn't he see it? Because some boys were wild was that a reason for him to be wild too? His mother went back to Edith's hair and eyed him from across the lobby—an unspoken sign that he should stay inside.

Martin watched his partner through the misty glass. To him the boy was a gamesplayer with guts. Martin's mother always saw danger and restriction first, the backside of a mysterious hand of fate about to strike.

But there were reversals. Moments when his mother's superstition and acceptance of the magical filled him with awe and a kind of horror. What if it were true that the Gypsy who appeared the day his great-grandmother died, and who had cursed her weeks

before for not offering a handout, really was a harbinger of evil? A
practitioner of potent Romany spells. This suggested the viability
of all kinds of magic. It suggested that his old grandfather's fear of
lightning was not unfounded. It might well have been some
retired necromancer, a Kabbalist on vacation, who brought the
storm up with wild *Gematria* and sent him out to stare at the
mountain in bare feet. These moments of doubt, though, did not
bring Martin any nearer to appreciating his mother's fears, to
actually knowing them and feeling the shape they formed in the
belly, the rush they set flowing in the head. The difference
remained. For Martin the storm was an event fit for exultation and
remembrance. For his mother it was a source of horror, one of the
many unknowable threats that came from beyond the pale and
was best forgotten.

And so their two worlds flickered, imposed themselves upon
each other like competing film reels cast on the same screen, never
complementing each other, always at odd angles. The ephemera of
one vision shifting to the ephemera of another.

Martin's heroes were movie people, scalped cowboys, the rough
men who rode in the rain and arrived at little wet western towns,
ready for action.

Martin's mother sometimes spoke of the one movie she had
seen in Warsaw, in a cinema her father derisively called a *Flim-
merkisten*—a flicker box—using the German to make the ritual
seem all the more dangerous and modern. The screen flickered so
much that her eyes hurt. And in the overstuffed seats, the uncomfortable patrons searched for a place where they would not be illuminated by the funnel of light that poured out of the projector.
Around them, endlessly, roared the sound of bad machinery.

Retelling Old Tales

The art of the elegant lie. Martin took this up when he realized that in the annals of emotional blackmailers he was a pip-squeak. A small-time player who could never match the skills of his mother or Edith. A good lie—well told and supported with the right gestures of mock-seriousness and hurt—would often buy a week or even a month of calm before the particulars of a disagreement came into the open.

Martin lied to his mother about his business. She knew it was the biggest and most successful funeral parlor in town, but she didn't know what sort of funerals were conducted there. His wife's funeral was taken care of by a competitor. At the time of her death, Martin's building was being renovated, transformed from a modest chapel into a very orange, wallpapered and lush arrangement of rooms that looked more like a hotel than a place of ritual. It was a place, Martin politely told his post-restoration customers, where one did not speak of death but of passing on to rest. Euphemism seemed to confuse customers enough that they almost forgot they were arranging an interment. It reminded them of holidays, of a long sleep on a grassy hill.

Martin was fortunate the funeral home was a long bus ride from his mother's house. It was in a corner of the downtown she never visited, imagining that only knife-wielding dope-taking young men roamed the treeless streets there. So Martin was able to tell her with impunity about his Jewish clientele (which was nonexistent) and the pious bare-walled ceremonies (which he no longer conducted) and his interest in musicless solemn reminders of the afterlife (of which of course he had none). He suspected she disbelieved him, but since she had no clear picture of the alternative to the kind of chapel she approved of, she was unable to express her doubts. What was unknown, unimaginable, could never be disapproved of with much vigor.

Martin's mother would have imagined the worst if she could have. And she would have been right. The funeral home sprawled over half a small city block. On the northern wall, in a stained glass pastoral that overlooked the parking lot, ducks floated in a pond among bulrushes almost as high as the sun. At the front of the building, a mass of geraniums were crowded into flower boxes, over-watered and over-fertilized, their odd fragrance mixed with the smell of rich loam. A white Cadillac was always parked in the U-shaped driveway, white rocks lined the walkway to the front door, a white knee-high picket fence surrounded the impeccable lawn.

Inside were photographs of the Queen, the present mayor of Calgary and the man Martin bought the business from, all in equally sun-washed and faded blues and greens. A plain brown cross—but no image of Jesus—was suspended on the wall at the front of the chapel. There was no organ. Martin had installed an elaborate stereo system and was collecting recorded versions of every hymn he could get his hands on. He thought of his collection as definitive. World class. He would have contacted the people who listed world records if he wasn't mortified by the thought of one of his mother's friends—old biddies all—picking up the record book at a supermarket counter and reporting his notoriety to his mother. Ah, the indignity of being undone by an old biddy simply because she's jealous that her son makes less money than her friend's son, leaving innuendo and gossip the most effective way of addressing the inequality.

Martin was also familiar with the obverse of the elegant lie—the celebration and embellishment of what little bit of the truth is attractive. "I celebrate," Martin might have said, if he were to lose all restraint and patience, "I celebrate myself for giving Edith a job. My manic unkind cousin eight or nine times removed, who is no good at anything except failed suicide attempts. An expert she is at oddities like swallowing hangers. Trying to hang herself with her shoelaces. My cousin, who is trying to become the first person to murder, unaided, with nothing but lunacy and ill will in her arsenal. To this person, I give a job." But he kept himself in line and said nothing of the kind as his mother asked careful hopeful questions about Edith's worth as an employee.

"But is she happy, Martin? Does she like working with you?"

"Have you ever known Edith to be happy?" This was a response of the inappropriate and ignorable kind.

"Does she come in every day?"

"I've told you she does."

"For how long?"

"A couple of hours. An afternoon sometimes if it's busy. There was just that one week when she was in the hospital." That one week followed Edith's most illustrious suicide attempt, which was as unsuccessful but much more dramatic than anything she had tried before. Its particulars included the taking of a handful of pills —not enough to be lethal but enough to send the taker shrieking up roadways in slippers and pajamas. Which is what Edith did until she reached the train tracks near her house where she lay down. She lay down but continued to scream until a couple out for a stroll passed by and dragged her off the rusty rails.

"You should keep more of an eye on her, Martin."

"Mother. If I saw any more of her, it would be me running up and down the street in my slippers."

Silence. A bee popped in the open window and headed for the ceiling. Martin watched his mother for a reaction, but she didn't appear to notice. A crab apple tree—the widowed mate of the one his friend had demolished—blocked his view of the yard. From where he sat at the table, he saw only a mass of green-yellow leaves, interrupted here and there by a shiny reddening piece of fruit. Somewhere in there, Martin expected, that thug of a cat was lurking. It was the essential alley cat, with a little brown moustache on its top lip and a brown mark to the right of its mouth that made it look like it was smoking a cigar. A patch was torn out of its fur, showing pink healing flesh below. Sometimes the cat greeted Martin on the front step and faced him down, as if some ransom were required before he could enter the house. Martin hated that cat. It reminded him of his mother's friends, peeking and pushing in where they didn't belong.

Martin made an effort to stop hearing his own thoughts and pay attention to what his mother was saying. But the conversation was so familiar he could follow it by its rhythm alone.

"But imagine what might have happened to her."

"Mother, I've told you a hundred times. Those tracks aren't used anymore. There's grass growing up between the ties that's as high as my hip. She would have starved there before she got hit by a train."

Martin's mother folded and unfolded and refolded a napkin that lay on the table in front of her. She concluded the familiar report. "You don't know. How could you know when a train comes by there? Have you stood there, day and night, to see? Grass and rust! A train can't go through grass and rust? I think of it all the time. I think of her lying down there like a mad woman with no one to help her."

Martin kept his thoughts to himself.

"She had trouble, trouble, trouble ever since she was engaged to that rotten man."

"You talked her into it, mother."

"But I thought she'd be better off. All her friends were getting married. That's what girls did then."

"Married drunks?"

The bee found its way into the bowl of the lamp that hung in the center of the ceiling. It bounced noisily around inside, finding no corners to settle in, no flat predictable surface to cling to. Martin's mother kept folding the napkin until it stood up, a thin paper accordion.

"You don't tell me everything, do you Martin?"

"What is it that I should be telling you?"

"Things about Edith. Why she never married that man. I shouldn't have to hear these things from strangers."

Martin heard the woman who lived upstairs making her way down the hall. His mother believed that this tenant, thirty-five years in the house and closer to her cats than anything else, was a troublemaker, a searcher in drawers. She even believed that through careful listening and note taking, Miss Duncan, a tried and true Scot, had learned Yiddish on the sly. Miss Duncan was in love with the other tenant, an old tired horse of a man with a good disposition and a huge belly who lived downstairs. Martin called him the basement man. His mother referred to Miss Duncan as *di oibeshte,* the one above.

Miss Duncan would be his excuse not to say anything more. He shook his head and pointed over his shoulder, as if he didn't want to be overheard. It was late afternoon. The sun came down the hallway, lying in dusty lines on the rug. Miss Duncan ducked into the bathroom. Out the door on the gray-painted front step, rose petals swirled in a private eddy the railing and the breeze made together. The street was all dust and filtered light; long shadows and rainbows hovered in the fans of water spraying from sprinklers. Martin remembered himself as a boy and realized none of this mattered to him then. No one could have stopped him long enough to make him pay attention to all the slow movement and light. The idea was to move quickly and not be seen. To build boxes and forts, to lay boards against walls that provided one with shelter and invisibility. Holes had to be dug for burying, warrens investigated for quarry, the wind and insects and dirt had to be caught in jars for the purpose of destroying all three. The challenge was to devise a mess that was one's own, controllable, the proof of power.

For timid playmates, those happy to leave things as they were, there were insults and the threat of indignities only a child could dream up. Once Martin and a friend filled a padded envelope with handfuls of blueberries, sealed it, mashed the contents carefully and mailed the mess to a boy who'd refused them a ride in his little pedal-propelled racer.

"If you won't tell me, I'll tell you myself what I've heard." Martin's mother stood behind him, arms crossed, pulling her sweater close around her shoulders. She raised her eyebrows, waited.

On the Way West

There's nothing to tell. There's nothing to tell. Just tell her there's nothing to tell, Martin repeated to himself as he watched the petals eddy on the shining paint. There's nothing to be gained from her knowing. Young people acted like that thirty years ago. I'm not the one to educate my mother. But it sounds as if she's already heard, which is beyond me. What does that mean—she shouldn't hear it from strangers? As if she meets people in the street who say, "Excuse me, I recognize you as Rivka Binder, the friend of Edith Simon, and I've heard a story about that young lady (hands coming up to a smiling mouth) that's a real pipperoo. A whopper." All this being incomprehensible to mother because she understands no slang of any era. Surely it wasn't one of her old biddies who uncovered the story, although they're just the type to scan the lists of gossip items in community newspapers about knifed pawnbrokers, abused dogs, robbed corner stores. They gather tales about other people's misfortunes the way some people collect stamps. A special page for the really gaudy items. A book for a nation's dead and dying, a catalogue of rape and ruin. One of the more illustrious snoops after family tragedy might well have befriended a policeman just to gather reports of cases the press wasn't interested in.

Then Martin felt the same jolt of fear the well-pressed coat sleeve at morning caused in him. The fear of reprimand and humiliation. The shame of being caught in the act, asleep at the wheel. He realized the elegant lie was not only in Edith's interest but in his own. He had played a part in the idiotic antics that preceded Edith's aborted marriage, and if someone had told his mother about the trip, she knew he had witnessed the worst of it. This would be a revelation too ugly to be lied about. Martin stifled his discomfort by concentrating on the more petty and petulant thought that his mother had no right, in his absence, to know his whereabouts. It was his job as protector and sender of fence builders to know where she was. When a phone call had not informed him of her full day's plans, he could just as easily imagine her walking one of the short blocks to the bank or shopping in one of the stores where she bought what she needed for the house. On rare afternoons, the most windless and sunny days, when nothing stirred the dust and the power cables hung perfectly still between light posts and garages, she would go for a walk. If there was ever a reason to find her, Martin knew exactly which streets to search. Even her Sabbath had become predictable, since she no longer felt strong enough to walk to synagogue alone. Every part of her life could be imagined from afar, even her faith. She performed her devotions at home, one chair turned out from the dining room table, a prayer book in her lap.

It is hard to get the full story, since over the years it has been told badly and lied about, forgotten and then resurrected by the few men who knew it, for the sake of self-aggrandizement, one-upmanship and to more or less kill time when there was nothing else to talk about. Edith pretended the whole episode never happened. Martin's mother knew nothing of it and was bluffing when she threatened to tell the story herself. One of the men who knew what had happened was dead. Another had moved with his bad heart and his money to California. That left Martin, bearer as usual of the burden. And he had Edith on hand, behind the front desk at his funeral home, as a daily reminder. She still dressed as she had when she was twenty-five, and wore her hair in an identical style, but she was much grayer and sadder than she had been then.

Edith never spoke about Jack Hansen. It was as if she had never met him. There were no photographs in her apartment of him or of herself at the age when she met him. She kept photographs of old friends and of her father. Of herself she kept only one lurid portrait, painted when she was eighteen, which showed her from the bust up wearing a red dress, her hair windswept around her face. Martin never saw Edith cast a glance at the portrait, but he suspected it was the only mirror she trusted. He had a recurring dream of her standing before it, studying the wind in her hair and the red silk straps on her shoulders. It was not a bad likeness— Edith was pretty as a young woman. But there was something garish and cartoony about it. It was over-romantic, showed too much glow (or mock glow) around the eyes, and the hair gave off a yellow shimmer: the subtle suggestion of a halo. Martin saw the portrait more than once in half-light, when his mother sent him over to drop something off for her. He could never find a light switch in Edith's front hall. He was sure she kept them all hidden behind wall hangings to foil would-be thieves. So he tripped in sometimes, with a carton of cigarettes or a case of toilet paper, to the rhythm of the stereo playing and replaying the last half-inch of silent vinyl (the tick–whir–tick Carl Perkins never knew he wrote) and looked into Edith's face—a gaudy icon presiding over the ashtrays.

That is the way she looked to him at the engagement party her friends threw for her. Posed, resplendent and utterly bogus. She came out of the hall with her chosen, who was eyeing not his wife but one of his cronies. She had a smile stretched over her face and a hairdo that wouldn't move in a hailstorm, and she seemed to be impersonating something hollow and wooden that belonged on the prow of a sailing ship.

"Do I make you happy?" she asked her mate once they were driving away from the waving crowd.

"Yah. You make me happy."

"Do you miss me when we're not together?"

"Why are you asking me that now, Edith? We just got engaged. We're never gonna be this together again."

This sounded to Edith like quite a sweet thing to say, and she slid over nearer to her partner. She really didn't know Jack Hansen yet. She had no idea what he planned to do with his life, but she did know that he was a good dancer, which was important. And more to her credit, she did not yet know that he was a drinker. Such an illustrious drinker that when his liver—shoelike and useless—quit on him years later, the doctors who examined Jack Hansen would declare it the most ravaged specimen they had ever seen. This was the kind of record that would have to go uncelebrated.

For an engagement gift Jack went out of his way to prove he was a sport. He rented a car and drove with Edith to Banff, which, he informed her, was such a classy place to go for a weekend that she should certainly feel lucky. Which she did. Counting telephone poles and watching for wildlife, her arm around Jack's neck as he cracked his gum and aimed for the lean prairie dogs that froze, dazed on the hot highway. She felt so lucky just to be there with him that she had almost no expectations for the coming days, which was good, since Jack had no intention of fulfilling any.

Their talk was limited to estimations about the weather, excited pleas from Edith to know if they were staying at the big hotel, and sharp replies from Jack assuring her that she'd find out when she got there. They had made a late start, and as the day wore on toward dusk, becoming moist and cool, the open vents at their feet filled the car with sweet breezes. Edith imagined teeming thickets by the roadside. Manic quacking and cackling, whining and skittering as hidden warrens emptied and laden swarming trees were abandoned under nocturnal cover. Edith was not exactly knowledgeable about the forest wildlife—bestiaries were out of style when she was a child. And in the spirit of endless possibility, with no hard facts to go on and time to kill, she improvised wildly. She imagined the countryside hid fish that flew, delivering letters splattered with primitive postage stamps; stunted white giraffes and slack-backed dogs; strange premodern shelled rock-climbers and slick oversized lizards with gaping mouths for heads. By the lakes she imagined long-beaked birds sifting the water for food while the trees, magical trees, offered up prickly pink gourds, sprigs of parsley as big as lettuce heads, fat leaking clumps of berries hanging on the thinnest possible stems.

For Edith, the Rockies and the stands of looming pine presented the entrance to a garden of earthly delights. A place where everything flowered, and a new discovery lurked behind each mileage marker. She felt sure her splendid El Dorado was not far beyond the next rest stop. And she held on to the hope that the western sky would keep its olive gray and crimson brilliance long after it had gone irreversibly shadowy and dark.

Jack's thoughts went toward the east, backward to a different garden of delights: the big headlights on Martin's convertible, the stars lying in a puddle on the pale blue hood. Jack wondered who Martin was bringing with him. He imagined the faces inside the car illuminated by oncoming headlights, smiles—expressions of boredom, the occasional leer all showing beneath eyes that searched the dark for the back end of his car. And Jack thought of the same faces searching for the back of his head, slick and rectangular beside Edith's hail-proofed hairdo. It pleased him to think his scalp was the object of a hunt. He liked being trailed by a car buried in the dark, eating up the highway at some unknowable distance. This was the sort of thing Jack could get excited about.

The arrangements had been made the day before at the Café

des Westens. It had been a bad afternoon. Two hard-up types had dined and dashed, and Ostrovsky spent the better part of the day in the back room hyperventilating, worn out after chasing the two lean thieves around the neighborhood—pointlessly. Both disappeared over fences, laughing, as Ostrovsky, 180 pounds of well-fed flesh, slammed off the loose boards and bounced like a circus performer.

Feeling vulnerable, a little unhealthy, two Clubhouse sandwiches in the hole, he had no patience for the regulars' usual banter. One of the men who'd hung around all afternoon, paying little attention to Ostrovsky's displeasure, was the local alderman, Smith, a round cigar smoker who kept his thumbs hooked in his suspenders, as if he believed this pose guaranteed him the trust of his constituents. Smith was dedicated to politics. He was practicing a good-hearted attitude in the hope it would get him on a postage stamp.

When Ostrovsky felt strong enough to stand, he made his way behind the countertop and poured himself a cup of coffee. Spread out on a tiny stool, Smith chewed on the end of an unlit cigar and snapped his suspenders. Ostrovsky stood across from him with his coffee and a sandwich he had saved from the lunch run.

Instead of reaching for his meal, Ostrovsky grabbed Smith's cigar out of his hand, shouting, "No smoking while I eat." He looked at the chewed end in disgust. "Or I'll call the cops. And after the cops come I'll have you shot. Take me about 30 seconds. And I especially can't stand cigars. You've got to buy a good Cuban cigar with no smell, not these cheap ones you smoke, Smith." Ostrovsky threw the cigar over his shoulder and it disappeared into the deep steel sink where he washed glasses.

The alderman acted as if Ostrovsky had offered him the warmest of compliments.

"You always were a card, Ostrovsky. Just tell me if there's anything wrong in the neighborhood. Sewers backed up—I'll send the right man over. Bad wires—just give me a call the day before the inspector's due. You know what they say about me: 'Smith is as straight as a summer's day.'"

"Long."

"What, long?"

"Long. Long as a summer's day. That's the saying." Al Shipman slouched with his face hidden in his hands.

"I don't get you, Shipman. You're always riding me. Your dad gets his zoning changes when he pays me. What have I ever done to cross you?"

"Nothing. Nothing, Smith. It's your suspenders. They give me a headache."

The door slammed behind them, and Martin crossed the room to the counter. He was a bit younger than the others, not yet as well established, but he was well liked—for his sense of humor and for being Ostrovsky's best friend—and his presence guaranteed the proprietor's toleration of their lounging, the endless cups of coffee they poured each other.

As Martin found himself a stool, a head turned and a hand shot out. Martin reached to shake it, and the man who offered his hand held on to Martin's, pulling him halfway off his stool.

"Howdy, relative."

"Hi, Jack."

"We're gonna be family soon."

"I know it."

"You don't sound too excited about the prospect."

"No, Jack, everything's fine. If you're what Edith wants, then that's good by me. But you make your own lives together. I don't want to pry."

Martin flinched, tried to peel Jack's fingers from around his.

"But I want to start things off on the right foot." Jack stood and put his arms around Martin and Al. Both men cringed beneath the seersucker embrace as Jack announced that everyone was invited to follow him to Banff to throw an unofficial pre-honeymoon celebration, providing him with entertainment if

Edith knocked off early. Martin pushed the man who looked most excited by the idea off his stool. Although Martin was not on friendly terms with Edith, already sick of her freeloading at the house, he felt his family's honor required some kind of response. This chivalrous act only served to raise Jack's plan out of the realm of hearty banter and dignify it as an imperative—a point of honor. Al Shipman, the brashest and richest of the men present, announced that when he felt like taking a cruise out of town, he took a cruise. And he didn't ask people if they thought this was a good idea or not.

As they argued over Jack's plan, Smith pulled himself off his stool, took the last sip of his cup of coffee and backed out of the action toward the door. He disappeared behind the coat rack, but reappeared, waving his arms and yelling, "Boys! Boys! Allow me to interrupt, only to pay Ostrovsky for my coffee. Ain't nobody around here gonna say that I get my coffee by favor of my constituents."

So the next day, as Jack and Edith drove west, three people rode in Martin's car, trailing them. In the front seat sprawled on the passenger side was the young man who asserted his right to cruise when he chose. This was Al Shipman, whose father began gathering oil leases before the war, making his son feel like the son of a robber baron among the sons of grocers. Al was preceded everywhere by word of his father's wealth as well as by a reputation so bad that for the most part only people more crooked than he was would have anything to do with him. Crooked card players were especially fond of Al because his wallet was always full of his father's money, and he was unable to remember the cards dealt from one hand to the next. Al seemed to feel that bravado shared out generously among his peers should be payment enough for his inability to win a game. Martin could not avoid him. Al owned the house where Martin and his family lived. And they had known one another since they were old enough to sit up on a rug and stare at each other. Al was like bad weather you got used to and even became a little fond of with familiarity.

Al was oblivious to the rumors that circulated about him. He scrambled in his memory the reports of afternoons when the roughest gamesplayer appeared in his father's office, catching the old man with his back turned, his hands buried in a box of receipts, and presented as his credentials a pistol. Sitting on a folded metal chair, a quarter the size of the seated backside, the visitor said, "Look, old man, you are old but not venerable. So I wouldn't consider it an affront to your dignity if I shot your son—who is a rat. And I'll do just that if he doesn't start paying his debts." The gun-wielder shifted to find the right roll on his rump to fit into the curve in the seat. The old man, still fiddling with his papers, took a quick look at the visitor, shrugging, "It's a small gun." The answer to this being, "You've got a small son." Which was a piece of information the old but not so venerable man agreed with wholeheartedly. He reached into a drawer, lifted the false bottom and produced the sum in question.

Al rode in the front seat of Martin's car, feeling like a dignitary on vacation. A superintendent of sums who had shut his ledger with the numbers in disarray and gone out for a laugh among friends. He wore one of his white suits with a brilliant red pouf in the breast pocket, his sunglasses on top of his head, buried in his thick black hair.

Martin drove. He had conceded defeat, accepted that Edith's first intimate outing with a man was fated to become a fool's parade and hoped that by being along for the ride he could prevent some of the humiliation Jack was arranging as a surprise. But add to this his knowledge that Al had acquired a friend for the trip, and that this friend was acquired—with no strings attached—at Al's expense for the duration of the weekend, and that Martin, who might be considered utterly normal in most regards, had an abnormally high interest in this kind of acquired yet expensive no-strings-attached type of friend.

She sat now in the backseat of his car, glorious mystery from the realm of bar stools and eleven o'clock dinners, dweller in the world of street-smart, wisecracking toughs, keeper of illicit gifts. She seemed to be spread out over a great deal of the backseat, which was no small feat. Parts of her lay up and along the top of the seat while others disappeared unseen below it. She sparkled like a gem show in a hotel lobby and wore something tight fitting and red that Martin could not confidently recognize as a long sweater or a short dress. Her name was Susan, and she was absolutely frightening.

As the drive wore on, Martin watched the part of her that was visible in the rearview mirror almost as much as he watched the road. It no longer occurred to him that the mirror was fixed on the ceiling to improve his view of what was outside the car. It was there to see the backseat, and he carefully adjusted its angle every twenty minutes, feigning unusual attention for the road. He covered himself as much as he could in the presence of beauty and danger. He kept his jacket buttoned and his tie pulled very close to his neck, never thinking of removing his shoes to give his feet air. If he had a coat he would have pulled it on and buttoned it. Another covering retained for the pleasure of obfuscation.

Al was offering up some characteristic truisms aimed at explaining why Martin should not—in situations where he felt himself compromised—let his conscience get the better of him. "It's going to get you," Al rambled, "into a hole. And you're going to lie in that hole for a while and think: this is a hole, but it's better than anything else because I'm being true to myself. But then the equation Being True to Myself Equals Being In a Hole will start to seem mighty depressing, and you will start to change yourself, so that you will be able to justify a climb out of that hole. And wherever you get to, you will be a different person by the time you get there. A different person altogether."

Martin had his window open partway, and the rush of air, sweet with the scent of pine, along with the flap of his tires and the odd sign that rushed by, helped him ignore what Al was saying. He imagined that the glare of headlights, caught for a moment inside the car, was really a flash of Susan's eyes. That the pine smell was her scent, the flapping of the tires a rhythm that she alone could count. And so he was hypnotized. A devotee who did not need to see the object of his adoration undertake any miraculous acts. His faith in her power and his fear of it were felt unquestioningly.

She was maintaining some terribly classical pose, like the daughters of Pharaoh in a drawing by Poussin, who sit, large and lambent, built as much of measured arches and golden triangles as the stairs and monuments they rest upon. She was not exactly sitting but not really reclining, and her face was a moveable mask, which looked haughty then bored, ecstatic then idiotic. Martin wished he could take impressions of her face as it shifted in the shadows, the blue night hanging behind her in the window like a perfect velvet curtain. He would put them on the wall in his room, clay frowns and grins, more unique than any other trophies. Never speaking, she was an oracle stuffed full of her own importance. An absolutely miraculous source of riddles.

As his attention to her grew, Martin felt himself shrinking, becoming gnomish, a bodiless entity. Shriveled at the wheel, he steered the car up the winding two-lane road in the dark that led past bungalows set back on treed lots, past a pancake house, a small motel, more bungalows and then the grounds of the hotel where Al thought Jack had rented a room. Martin grumbled and groaned, complaining that Edith would recognize his car. He turned off his headlights in the parking lot.

"You're gonna hit something," Susan announced, lighting a cigarette and filling the car with her first hearty drag.

"Or something's going to hit you, Martin. You're the biggest thing out here." Al had his arm hanging out the window and was slapping a rhythm on the door.

"Cut that out, Al. Christ. We shouldn't even be up here."

"We've got to see if their car's here. I can barely believe that Jack sprung for a room in this place."

"There's the car." Martin pointed at Jack's rent-a-car. It was parked, half-tipped, on the embankment. "So let's get out of here."

Al started to laugh, alternating heaves and groans, wheezing, slapping his hands together. He looked over his shoulder. "Pretty funny, eh Susan? This guy is pretty funny." Al kicked the floorboards and clapped some more. "Just drive, Martin. You're here to drive. You're the chaperon." This gave both Al and Susan a thrill, and they whooped and coughed and spat all over each other all the way back down the dark winding road into town.

They checked into a motel, chosen by Martin for the sake of its parking lot, which was hidden behind one wing of the building. Al kept putting his arm around Susan and crooning, "Our honeymoon, darling. A honeymoon room just for us. With the mountains and the mountain air and the mountain sky and our own chaperon." They alternated between singing and laughing as Martin tried to discover which key opened the door to their room. He pushed the door open and hung on to it as Al and Susan squeezed by him, arm in arm.

The room looked very small and a bit like a renovated stable, with its wooden floors—long thick planks with uneven gaps between them. If you looked through the gaps, Martin thought, you would find a wealth of pencils, hairpins, dimes, paper clips, matchbooks, bus tickets. A mass of things thin enough to be carried carelessly in back pockets. And the badly laid floorboards reminded him of a hastily built stage, a covering thrown down to hide the remains of previous shows. There might be more down there than bits of stationery and spare change. He wanted to put an eye between two planks, set a table lamp on the floor to cast a beam into the gap. Watch the light pouring over buried ruins, uncovering what slept beneath the step of fat black mountains that cut triangles out of the sky.

These excavations would have to be carried out in careful stages. Work on one city must not destroy what lay beneath it.

There were distractions. One of Martin's companions had turned on the radio that was screwed to the nightstand. Al insisted on a particular Calgary station, so the reception was bad, the announcer's voice rising up over the foothills and then dipping below them, swallowed in the winds on the flats. Songs by little-known British crooners, by Frank Sinatra and by Dean Martin stuttered on and off. The Mills Brothers sang for a moment about the Alamo until the weather over the foothills interfered, and the machine gun growl of static took over.

Martin sat on a chair in the corner, deeply relieved that Al was being kept busy on the bed. From there he was unable to square his big shoulders in the door, drop his sunglasses onto his nose and announce, "We're going Martin. It's time Martin. No more brooding. Jack's waiting."

It seemed that the threat of these commands had passed. Martin let himself doze off with his legs crossed, his elbow on one knee, his chin on his fist. He slipped through a knothole in the floorboards and rode the bank of russet light that dripped down through the cracks over layer upon layer of buried cities. The city closest to the surface was his own. His hometown. He marched through it, counting the silver blue living room dramas that lined the side streets. He counted the stands of poplars along the boulevards, the black and green cars pulled up tight to the curbs, the shadows, even in nighttime, thrown between the neatly kept homes. These were black and white streets. Streets for ambling down, driving along slowly. Streets where dust blew up from the gutters and in from the outskirts. On them nothing exceptional was seen—except once—when Martin broke his stride to stare through a basement window that framed a woman, naked, half-bending to hang her hair beside her so it could be brushed. He liked to zigzag from one side of the street to the other, mapping new circuits on the familiar grid.

Below this city was another darker version of the same place where the wide roads and gaps between houses were replaced by thin airless alleys. Familiar houses leapt skyward with a thousand more peaks and windows than Martin was accustomed to. The corner stores and laundries vanished in favor of saloons and gaming houses. Useless outposts without a single familiar face, where codes of behavior were unknowable. Unlearnable. Standing in a rashly opened door, one saw only a mass of heads, men's heads, hatless, bent over tables full of crackling and whistling game pieces. The steam from an unseen kitchen rolling along the ceiling, down the walls, the source of slim little waterfalls on the windows. All heads turning to greet the visitor, game pieces caught in midair like sluggish birds, and then all becoming normal again when the figure in the doorway is judged to be an outsider. A newcomer undeserving of attention. And outside in the thin airless alleys, more men wearing hats and trench coats—presumably the costume of some hermetic order—stand beside concrete pillars. Waiting. Lapels in disarray. Hatbands full of sweat. Hands fidgeting deep in pockets. Tapping worn soles on the ground, which lies, barely settled, over another city. An unrecognizable place. Purely imagined. Built of peaks, tipped oblong rooms full of high windows hung with flowing white curtains that billow in the wind. Billow endlessly, forming shimmering white depths that are unnavigable. The only ocean without a coastline. Winding alleys lit by gaslight lead to the clapboard hut where the most masterly mind in town keeps his sleeping treasure. Amidst empty shelves. Crooked windows. Lamps send wild diagonals like lightning strokes down walls and across the inlaid floorboards. From the outskirts of this city can be heard the groans and cheers of a carnival crowd. Like automatons at a witches' Sabbath, circling trees, following banners raised so high they cannot be seen, fair-goers celebrate through the night. Hands raised—two-fingered, three-fingered, four—assenting to anything. Following the orders of puppets, the decree of the hurdy-gurdy. "It is our time now!" the crowd chants, as papier-mâché and cotton, the trill of the music box, send them lurching one way and then another. Their high dimpled hats and braided hair flying, mouths gaping in the breeze, until the fine round moon goes down in the brightening sky, the clouds, gray below and white above, shuttling by like trains. Then the fair-goers go marching home, keeping their eyes on the broken flagstones, never seeing the lamplighter—shoehorned into his skintight black uniform—as he goes from lamp to lamp dousing each hissing yellow flame. In the empty homes coffee is boiled until it is burnt over a coil of flame. Stoves stand cold and white, icebergs with nothing to hide. The day begins its fine routine: women and boys stand on balconies, their arms dangling over the rail, jackets buttoned in the cool morning breeze. Partners make plans, whispering on the roadside and gesturing as little as possible, eyes still, so as to give nothing away. Teams of wild horses, ill-equipped, too muscular for their trade, pull open carriages up and down the dusty streets. Tall-hatted coachmen sleep at the reins. They rouse themselves only to apply a resounding smack with a whip that sets the beasts howling and racing all the more out of control. And behind heavy doors, in dark rooms, little men fall over one another, pile up like cords of wood before a stage on which a woman in a broad skirt affects poses meant to convey desire, distress, desperation, dreaminess. The woman's hair is dark and cut straight across her forehead. Her face is made up, black around the eyes. She is a mock-goddess with a concertina. The little men think only of how there are rooms full of such women, on divans, stretching their legs and tying their hair in loose knots. The men pile up and sleep at the foot of the stage, enraptured by their dreams until early evening when the moan of the carnival wakes them again, and they join the procession back out to the clearing where they put on their dimpled hats, hang open their mouths and join their braided-haired mates until the moon goes down.

This moonlight descends to another buried city, the mate, the sister, the opposite of Martin's hometown—his mother's. Buried like a corpse, a corpse beneath a pile of corpses, lies his mother's birthplace. The forever full moon comes up over it and sits in the branches of an elm tree. The streets are silent, silver-pale and still. In the market square and on Polish streets, the trees hang over the roadway, as if their branches are headed earthward, trying to keep their distance from the sky, its slate gray at morning, its blue at midday. On Jewish streets there are no trees. There are wooden buildings, a few made of stone. Someone is up early to carry water. A lone man is seated on a bench. A porter rushes by, the thick rope he will use to bind his first load tied around his waist. It is either Tuesday or Friday—a trade day—and the peasants ride their carts into town from the outskirts, bringing wheat, baskets of fruit, loads of screaming geese, ducks, chickens and turkeys. Those on foot carry baskets full of butter and cheese, earthenware pots full of cream and mounds of berries that arrive half-flattened, squashed under their own weight.

The entire town comes out of doors. The hurdy-gurdy man takes requests from children who gaze down at him from second story windows. A crowd gathers to see what the market offers. Men and women inspect bottles of honey wine to see if the stock is the right color. They dip their fingers in the brine where sour pickles and herring swim, squeeze white rolls under the scornful eye of shopkeepers.

In the late afternoon a whistle signals the arrival of the express train carrying the prized bundles of newspapers. A train arrives at the station every two hours, day and night, bringing the rest of the world into town, taking away those who wish to see the rest of the world. Travelers board the express train to Warsaw, which is not easily mistaken for the local or the freight train. Still, there is a newness about the machinery that inspires fear. And there is an ignorance about it that leads to bizarre conclusions. Periodically one Jew sits at the depot throughout a long afternoon, wondering why he has not yet reached Warsaw. Travelers pass him, patient in the sun, and greet him. Martin's mother does this repeatedly in her buried city. She greets the seated wayfarer as she walks with her sister to the station where the rails leap south toward Warsaw. On either side of the railway tracks are rolling fields dotted with yellow groundsels, camomile, blue cornflowers.

Back in town the Alexandrover Chasidim dispute and implore, setting long white-tableclothed lunches out in the sunlight, shouting their interpretations, derivations, wild renditions at one another while the younger initiates huddle behind their seated masters, hoping to overhear an inspired word, a mind-turning dictum.

Of Martin's buried cities this one is the noisiest. It harbors the most memorable characters. In the sunlight, arms waving, young men exchange stories that are known to all but retold and reexamined like talismans for new facets or flaws.

"It is said," one says to another, "that the mountains were not always here." To this a nod. "That they are a recent creation. A miraculous growth." And here the listener picks up the tale, gesturing mountainward. "The townspeople were making plans for a terrible weekend of slaughter. And they met in a church to discuss the possibilities." "But the Lord broke the earth under them," the other continues, "and as they were swallowed, covered, swept away, the mountains came up like stones in a graveyard." "And if you listen," continues the other, nodding, "with your ear to the ground, there still can be heard the mutterings and mumblings of their plans."

Nearby, as a counterpoint, two men describe what was discovered in a dead man's house. A manuscript full of calculations, *Gematria* and acronyms gathered to help predict the coming of the Messiah.

"A *meshugas.*" The work is dismissed with the wave of a hand. "Old Wolf Breindele made the same predictions every Rosh Hashanah. And every year he had to push the date off another year and make up ridiculous reasons why he was mistaken again."

"Watch your tongue. Saying these things could bring bad luck. Speak well of a dead man. His predictions for this year have yet to be proven wrong."

"This is a game you play, honoring a dead fool's word! You, would you run with suitcases packed to the station for the next turbaned preacher who comes to town?" The two descend into wild deprecation, expressions of disgust, waving hands and shaking heads, each posing as a god of judgment.

While all this is discussed and legends are repaired, the train begins its progress toward Warsaw. Commissionaires wrap themselves in heavy blankets and snooze. Boxes are opened. Tin containers, which hold a hard-boiled egg, a bit of herring, a flask of brandy, are brought out from under the seats. Passengers marvel at the countryside as it is tripled and quadrupled in the windows of the rail car. Left behind at the station, the patient but ill-informed Jew, having not arrived at Warsaw once again, makes his way back down the road to town. He passes the fields where witches were burned and beheaded, and the church, behind which an ancient garden is hidden, formally planted with towering trees and a maze of shrub and flower beds. Hidden in the secret corners of this garden are boys and girls who do not think of the verdicts meted out to witches or Jews or thieves, who are not concerned about the arrival of the next train, and who are not interested in blowing on the back feathers of a chicken to see if the bird is plump. They are busy hiding in the bluebells. Burying themselves in shadow.

On the Floor

There was a loud rap on the door. Martin's chin slipped off his fist, his elbow slipped off his knee. His legs came uncrossed, and he kicked the floor as he stopped himself from sliding off the chair. Jack was in the room, holding a glass of something above his head. He turned to Martin, with the glass aloft, and bowed, pouring most of its contents on the floor. Then he took a step forward and slipped in what he'd spilled. But Jack was a good dancer, swift and sure on his feet, which was the only good thing that could be said about him, and he did some kind of two-step and regained his balance.

Martin thought immediately of Edith, alone at the big hotel in one of the stale badly decorated rooms with a mosquito smashed on a yellow wall, its guts full of blood trailing half a foot behind it, a sock hiding under the double bed.

Susan was sitting on the edge of the bed, her ever-present cigarette burning down between two fingers. Once Jack had quit hopping, he began to perform for her. He took one of her hands in his, caressed it, kissed it, got down on his knees as if to propose marriage and sang rather sweetly with the radio:

> Till then,
> My darling, please wait for me
> Till then.

Al threw himself down in an armchair and mumbled about getting himself a drink. Martin was entranced by Jack's display. It was clownish. As Jack fawned, Susan withdrew from him, half-flattered, half-disgusted by his antics. And Martin was more than pleased with her rejection of his affections. He redrew it within the terms of an obsession that was growing within him. He felt a strong attraction—not for clowning—but toward worship, veneration. And though he wanted most to despise Jack, to undo the idiot drama he was performing for Susan behind Edith's back, he felt a maddening desire to take part in it himself. He would be a worshiper before a queen and, more than this, a groveler who could not lie low enough or touch his forehead to the ground enough times to express his devotion.

Jack stayed on his knees, and Susan loomed up over him, her chin upturned, a smile on her face and a bit of a quiver on her lip that Martin took at first to be a sign of desire and then one of disgust. He felt ashamed. Ashamed and enraged because he found the scene so compelling, and he went into the bathroom to hide from it. But the first thing he noticed in the darkened room once he'd shut the door was the grate covering the heating duct. Through it light shone from the bedroom, falling in a pattern of elongated yellow Xs on the linoleum. Martin bent to look closer and saw that the grate on his side matched a grate on the other side of the wall. He imagined a view of Susan from the ground up and got down on his elbow and hip, lay with one cheek on the floor, the other streaked with shadowy Xs, and looked out of the dark into the neighboring room. He peeked through a screen of dust and sand and unidentifiable husks that were piled at the edge of the vent.

From the other room he heard Al yell, "She's not here to keep you company, you engaged pig."

Martin felt the vibrations of someone's footsteps with the cheek he pressed against the floor.

"What do you mean by that, Al?"

"I mean," Al shouted, "that previous to this day you were just a pig. Now you're dignified. You're an engaged pig."

Martin shifted himself to try to get a view of something other than the bottom of the bed. He saw the legs of the night table and the bottom six inches of Al's white pant leg.

"If I'm so bad, Al, how come you hang out with me?"

"It's a small city. There's not a lot of variety."

"Oh, really?" Someone was pacing back and forth, making as much of a military operation of his movements as possible—heels ringing, rhythm almost perfect.

"I don't have to take this from you, Al. We don't owe you anything. Just because your father was the first Jew in town to buy a Stetson and sell oil bonds."

Al laughed, the sound of it coming from somewhere near to where Martin lay. "I don't know, Jack, if you've got anything to teach us about good behavior, seeing as how you just got engaged, and you're over here to see what I picked up on Third Avenue."

"Hey." The floor vibrated, and there was a short sharp sound like an axe hitting cordwood. Martin caught a glimpse of Susan's heels swinging off the bed onto the floor.

"Just a figure of speech, Susan. Christ. I'm trying to get a point across."

Jack misinterpreted this remark as a return to good humor and went back to his clowning, singing, paying no attention to what was accompanying him on the radio:

> Till then, my darling
> Please wait for me
> Till then. . . .

But the second verse was interrupted by a loud thud. Martin thought of a body falling off a garage. Then there was a louder more complicated noise, as if something many-sided and heavy had hit the floor. This was followed by groaning and banging, the scuffle of shoes being dragged around the room, something sliding slowly off something else, then a crash.

Martin had every intention of getting up and doing something. The thought of Al and Jack beating each other senseless was not such a bad one, but it was Martin's car that would have to carry them, leaking and spitting up blood, to the hospital up the hill. And the hotel room was in his name. Things were not so good with him that a bill for broken furniture, carpet cleaning and repainting could be absorbed for the sake of a good story. He would have gotten up, wanted to get up, assured himself it was the right thing to do, yet he couldn't. Because Susan had stepped into view, a colossus staring down on the fight that he could hear but not see. Martin was frozen, Xs on one cheek, the cold linoleum anesthetizing the other, his surreptitious worship—hosannas before the unknowing idol—too much to forego. He nearly had to stand on his head to set himself at the angle that offered the fullest view. Susan was repeating, "Stop it guys. Come on, stop it," but her tone betrayed a halfheartedness, as if she believed that the rule of decency obliged her to say something even if she had no allegiance to either battler.

This went on for some time: Martin on his head, his knees in the air, his toes extended for support. Susan wavered in and out of view, a hesitant referee looking for cheap shots. Jack and Al smashed each other into furniture and dragged each other across the floor, polishing it for the first time in years, until the banging on the door sounded above the noise of shoulders hitting floorboards, and all four participants paused long enough to hear a voice yell, "You in there. Open up. Open up, you clowns." The room got so quiet Martin could hear himself breathe. Then he heard a match hiss alight, Susan's throaty drag, and a persistent clicking—a sound like marbles make when they're shaken in a bag.

Martin came out of the bathroom, fixing himself in the way he always did when he was nervous. He smoothed his hair, chewed at a finger nail. Al held Jack by the shirt front, getting ready to slam him like a side of beef. The doorknob fell into the room, little screws and washers rolling all over the floor, which the incoming pair of policemen stepped on. Al looked down at Jack where he hung a foot off the wooden floor. "Looks like your fiancée's going to spend the weekend alone, friend."

Martin tried to appear ingenuous at first and half-shouted, "What are you doing here? Are my lights on? Did I park in a No Parking Zone?"

"Quite a party you're having here." One of the cops stared at Jack where he hung. "How would you folks like some free accommodation?"

Two

In Midsummer

"I have left." Max puts his knapsack down by the bed.

"Oh, you have, have you?"

"I have left." The declaration sounds less convincing the second time around.

"Who says you've left?"

"I do."

"If you've left, why are you still talking about it?"

"What do you mean?"

"If you had left, if you were completely here with me," Sara moves, adjusts her foot, which is hidden under her tailbone, "then you wouldn't be announcing 'I have left!'"

Max sighs. "Maybe I haven't left." The words sound empty once Sara has thrown them back in his face. She has a knack for bouncing things off him in this way, for mimicking him in a tone that makes what he's said seem boorish and pointless.

"Now that you've left, do you think you'll have to keep on leaving or will this do it for you?"

Max is helpless before Sara's sarcasm. He trusts her instincts too much to argue with her. There is no reliable line of defense.

He moves over to the window and pushes the green cloth that hangs as a blind away from the glass. The afternoon light pours in and turns the walls from gray to yellow, the carpet from gray to green. Sara's cat sits on a high-legged table beside the window casement, its head turned quizzically toward Max and the bars of sunlight. It seems to order, by the serious look in its eyes and the angle of its head, that he put the curtains back.

Max stands with his legs apart and his arms lost under the folds of cloth. "Go to hell, Bosco."

"Don't tell the cat to go to hell."

"Look at it's eyes, Sara. It's evil. I'm just telling it to go home."

Sara does not notice the light. She sits at a desk piled high with files and notebooks. An adjustable desk lamp casts a yellow circle over her work. Max bends into the light to kiss her and steps back into the gloom.

On the way over to Sara's, Max felt as if he were someone with something important to say. A man with an idea. Now he considers that his confidence was nothing more than the product of an afternoon of self-deception. This kind of doubt attacks him whenever Sara withdraws her approval. Her confidence and calm overwhelm him, to the point that he has begun to suspect that behind her quizzical smile lurks a secret. She seems to be training her features—her huge eyes, her mouth, the two deep lines that run from her nose down to her chin—to hold some inscrutable expression. Max feels too loud, too anxious, too young around her, a little like a schoolboy being taught how to act in good company.

The cat jumps off the table and alights near Sara's feet. It reaches out one paw as if to examine for reflexes and leaps onto the desk, resting on a sheaf of files, where it moves its front paws up and down in a marching kick, warming up its chosen seat.

Max sits on the bed and looks around the room, feeling very ineffectual, like Sara's shadow. It is difficult work to keep up with the books she reads, the movies and music she insists he share with her. And she has a raft of friends who intimidate him, though he feels duty-bound to get to know each of them. Many are artists or glorious dilettantes who do very little with their day, drink like demons, rent studios in granite buildings for the love of bad plumbing and classic architecture.

They seemed somehow invincible, these rebels, though they gagged on the riot that drink was causing in their stomachs and rarely had money for rent. Their talk sent Max on excursions to the public library because they dropped words like dada and deconstruction, and he was embarrassed as he faded into the woodwork of one conversation after another. He was a dullard when it came to aesthetics. A deadbeat during arguments concerning the radical left. And he was young still. He looked like almost any young man on the street who had not yet found his way.

Max tried to affect their style with no success. He couldn't drink at their speed or blow smoke out his nose. He was not overly interested in clothes or the latest band everyone was listening to.

But he could read up on things. In the downtown library he found a white-topped table that sat all day in the sun. Max waged an ongoing battle with the other patrons who drew the blinds to keep the room cool. He usually outsat them, fluttering his pages, cracking sunflower seeds and humming to himself until he was left alone, free to run the dusty Venetian blinds up to the ceiling.

Max liked the heat. He sat in the patch of sunlight that fell on the table and waited for the twin trickles of sweat that ran down the insides of his arms. He liked the dusty wind and the city's absolute languor as it dozed through the dry dead summer. Summer had grabbed hold of the city in May and tightened its grip as the months passed. By July a fine layer of silt had settled over Calgary's entire sunbaked sprawl. The trees were hung with limp shapeless leaves. They clung to branches like bits of trash put there as a joke. The Elbow River, through most of its course, was no more than a trickle surrounded by a few square yards of pebbles, and at a few spots it disappeared, becoming nothing more than a subterranean mud flow. As the grass thinned and flowers shriveled and fell over in the wind, there seemed to be nothing but dust in the world. The air was an architecture of dust. The ground was a deep solid pool of it. The city was an unpredictable mirage supported by dust. Rivers of ants ran everywhere through the failed earth. Little motionless children lay prostrate in the heat, their excitement stifled in the swirling air. And the whole city smelled of weed killer, since nothing desirable was growing, and all the undesirable species—those capable of taking root in a sand dune—were being exterminated with fanatical care. A hot wind howled endlessly, blowing a mixture of 2-4-D, car exhaust and sand around cracks in windows, down chimneys.

Men loosened their ties, pushed their suit coats as far back on their shoulders as propriety allowed. Women pulled at bra straps, imagining an undress that would put an end to their sweating and itching. There was no comfortable way to carry oneself in a dead zone where everything was shriveling up and blowing away and where regular business was only being done as a front, in a half-hearted attempt to prove that man could still be productive while the desert crept around his work.

The city became a carnival of bright hot days that seemed to invite calamity. Forests on the outskirts burst into flame. An unusually hungry band of locusts was roaming the southern middle of the province, getting fat on everything the wind hadn't blown away. Hysterical comparisons were made between the present situation and the ten plagues that humbled Pharaoh. Newspaper headlines were even more colorful than usual. There was something compelling about the way the heat changed people's lives. It distorted the conventional world just a bit, set everything off balance. Sara did not miss the opportunity to draw Max's attention to the fact that the city was being swallowed up by the wilderness—a wilderness he could walk into, out of the world of filial responsibilities, bouquet arrangements, limousine rental and maintenance. It was time he began to see things differently, to accept not the usual landscape but the one that hovered, wobbly and unclear, in the pillars of heat that shivered by the roadside. Max decided it was time to make a change.

Sara agreed. She told him it was high time he stopped living for his father's needs, whether the old guy was a widower or not. It was high time he moved out of his father's apartment and stopped worrying about whether he really wanted to inherit his father's business, which may well be the most successful funeral home in town, but who wanted to make a living from offering grieving customers a choice between mahogany, pine or the brightly colored porcelain jar used for cremation?

She had a point. Max was not drawn to funereal drama, not even to being the maestro of such undertakings. But Sara did not match her insistence that he abandon his family responsibilities with any suggestion of what he was fit to pursue, and he felt a blindness, even a touch of sadistic pleasure in her advice. When Sara talked about his future she reminded him of a swimming instructor he'd had as a child, who threw uncooperative students into the deep end, yelling *Swim! Swim!* pretending that something was being accomplished as the thrashing body sputtered and sank. Max felt somehow sunken and sputtering as his plans became more entwined with Sara's. As she drew him to her, away from family, friends and familiar places, he did not find that he exchanged a closeness with past things for a closeness with her. He only became more curious and obsessed. Was this love?

Rooms

Sara lives in a huge apartment in an old house off Seventeenth Avenue. A bay window facing the roadway is kept blacked out by blinds. A big poplar tree arches over it, dropping a snowfall of fluff and burst husks all through spring.

Her rooms, through every season, remain autumnal, silver gray, brown and dimly lit. The carpet, the walls and the ceiling are all fading at different rates. The apartment has the dappled shades of a bank of turning leaves. The walls are covered with old-fashioned patternless wallpaper, the kind of textured disguise that is put up to cover the badly plastered rotten walls beneath. Bosco the cat vanishes and reappears before this yellow and brown backdrop, blending into his surroundings as if by instinct.

In her bedroom Sara keeps a big wardrobe packed full of dresses and shoes. On the backside of one of its wooden doors is a long thin mirror, old enough that its silvering has deteriorated so that the reflection it offers is sprinkled with dark pockmarks, strange shapes like undiscovered continents. In addition to the bed is a divan that reminds Max of Dr. Freud's couch. It is so thin and has such a strange arrangement of contours that he finds it almost impossible to keep from rolling off it. In the corner, on top of a wooden chest, is an old-fashioned shaving bowl with a matching china pitcher.

Max has never heard Sara voice an opinion on why she chooses to live in such a place. He has never heard her say, "I love this place," or "I hate this place," or even, "I'm so tired of this place." And he has never heard her make a suggestion about what could be done to improve it. She seems to be carefully maintaining the rooms as if some kind of theater is being played out in them that requires only one set, one mood, one unmoving collection of shadows.

Sometimes they spend the afternoon there, Sara flipping endless games of solitaire on a little red and white card table, Max rummaging through her bookshelves to see what there is he hasn't heard of. She indulges her habit of telling him things while he indulges his of being told.

"That plant over there," she announces, without lifting her head to indicate where there is, "blooms every twenty years." She lays down the final piece in a pyramid of diamonds and hearts.

"Couldn't it be, Sara, that there's just not enough light in here, ever, and the thing will never bloom?"

"No, no. Really. This is its year."

"How do you know?"

"The woman who gave it to me said so. She said to put oranges beside it. That they would speed it up."

Max accepts this on faith or at least supposes that if this method does not actually work, it has at least two believers, which is something. Sara is the keeper of hundreds of similarly bizarre bits of information. An arcanum of knowledge out of which she draws an endless catalogue of stories and spells, accounts of historical events and scientific discoveries that she uses to shroud the most mundane things in obscure and possibly useless allegory. She is a competent reader of emblems and coats of arms, adept at the Tarot, an explicator of birthstones. She knows of a thousand flowers that stand for something: rosemary for remembrance, pansies for thought, fennel and columbines, herb of grace o' Sundays. There was a code to be read in every lazy flower bed. A wino passed out in a bar was likely to prompt a report on the effect of curare on the action of motor nerves (it kills by paralyzing the lungs). A routine choice at an ice cream stand might lead to a lengthy dissertation on the Neapolitan school (artistes who sensualized themes biblical—Belshazzar in Dionysian dress, Lazarus, just risen, already lusty). Discussions about contemporary politics were routinely undermined, waylaid and turned into forums for discussing the patriotic excesses of Garibaldi and Gambetta, the exploits of Mazzini (snubbed by Marx in front of a room full of red celebrities at the First International). In her parents' generation she would have been criticized for her eccentric habits. Five hundred years before her time, with the right combination of coincidence and ill fortune, she might have been burned as a witch.

It is Sara's independence he finds so compelling and, in its own way, unnerving. Even in the work she chooses, she is the paragon of free lancers, a despiser of bosses and the routine of nine-to-five days. Her most recent assignment came to her by way of a well-known polling agency, which, Max has discovered, amounts to nothing more than a glitzy office with pastel prints on the walls in a downtown office tower where a man in a suit keeps a Rolodex with phone numbers for his roster of itinerant researchers, his team of writers and painters and nonjoiners who take care of the agency's assignments in cheap rooms and on sticky café tables. By Friday she must present a report commissioned by none other than the Tattooists League of Calgary—a guild of craftsmen who feel their trade's reputation has suffered in recent years, has been demeaned to the point that a tattoo is attractive to no one but sad outcasts, rebels without a cause. The head office has snowed her under with reports, loaded her down with wall-sized charts and demographic maps supplied by the league's desperate executive.

From all this doubtful data, she must answer certain age-old questions, such as, what does the average man and the average woman think when they hear a tattooist has moved in next door? And if tattoo parlors operated like fast food outlets, in tiled, brightly lit mall storefronts, would they attract a better clientele? And further, what could a broad "Get-to-know-your-local-tattooist" campaign do to affect the dismal straits of the proud wielders of needle and ink? And finally there was the ultimate mystery: why was it that every tattoo parlor in every city in the world found its way to the red-light district?

Sara has gotten nowhere with her collection of Venn diagrams and market prediction curves. There isn't much you can do with a failed scarification ritual. She has discovered that Edwardian ladies were in the habit of placing tattoos in inaccessible places. Egyptian princesses, undressed for the last time when the resin and plaster came off their mummified remains, were revealed to have fancied certain elegant designs. But Sara can't see how these oddities will tease a prairie market.

Max knows more than he would like to about this project because Sara tried to enlist his help, telling him this could be their first real collaboration. He'd made the mistake of mentioning that Ostrovsky's father had worked as a tattooist when he first immigrated to Canada, and Sara wonders if there is something in this she could use—a campaign based on the tattoo as an emblem of the early frontier, of personal freedom and individuality. She is drawn to the image of a Jewish cowpoke, new to the cultural mosaic, his beard neatly trimmed, a new name issued to him by a pair of dour immigration clerks who agreed that Judah was the name of an ancient people but not the name of a living person. Max is under the impression that Ostrovsky has had his fill of interviews, so he has ignored Sara's pleas for help, telling her over and over, "He's a restaurateur, not a historian, Sara. Leave him alone."

Sara has lived in Calgary for two years, having abandoned her home in Montreal for a job she ended up turning down when she arrived in town. But she knows more than Max about the city's history and civic politics. She is a more reliable authority on which way one-way streets run. Whenever an old-timer appeared in the *Herald* obits, Sara knew more details than the newspaper. She broke the spell of disinterested columns—listing which years the man worked in the Turner Valley oil field, how his company fared during the big bust years—with anecdotes about the big open car he drove through town, steer horns on the hood, his white Stetson catching stray leaves, rain, dust. Sara didn't read up on local personalities the way her friends might have—to slam their kind of capitalism, their rape of the land, trading the Cree whiskey and guns for a birthright worth half a century's wealth. She was in simple awe of the tale. With enough detail and embroidery, any man's life became as big and gaudy as a cathedral, a beautiful false front propped up on two-by-fours. You could step into it and lose yourself.

To lose yourself. To tip the day sideways and treat it like a cheap souvenir city under glass that can be shaken so snow falls and settles on it. To take any distraction as a respite from the inner dance, the endless angst and concern, the useless crapola of conscience. To watch the funny ersatz snow settle and glitter under glass and be content. This was Sara's finest accomplishment. And it was how to do this that Max most wanted to learn from her. He didn't mind hearing about the Turner Valley, dada, the Neapolitan school and all Sara's other pet subjects, but he hoped she would teach him how to lose himself. He wanted to learn how to lie in her yellow catacombs like a corpse at noon without thinking about finding a job. How to feed the cat without considering it a waste of time. The whys and hows of solitaire, diary writing, aimless walks. How to abandon a family. It had been happening slowly since they met: he hadn't lost himself yet, but he was not quite himself either.

Max's father was not pleased. Martin wanted him at the funeral home, learning the trade. Learning what? How to embalm octogenarians and accident victims? No. How to drive the big Cadillacs up narrow streets without clipping road signs? No. How to comfort the bereaved? No. All this was already being done very well by reliable employees. Then what was it? Why was he needed as an accomplice?

Still, his father seemed divided, halfhearted in his efforts to sell Max on the thrills of husbanding a mortuary. And halfhearted as well in his attempts to get Max to stop seeing Sara, who was obviously a first-rate candidate for the role of bad influence, because Martin appreciated the companionship they shared. He liked to hear about the mornings they spent having breakfast out, exchanging sections of the newspaper. He liked to pick the two of them up and take them to parties so he could hear them argue about whom they liked and who had gotten drunk and acted like an idiot. He seemed to gain unbounded pleasure from knowing that they had each other, for Martin was very alone. So alone, Max thought, that his father might one day be overcome by it.

Martin was a little like a shell-shocked man whose attention would always be centered on the one deafening heartbreaking event that changed his life. His wife's death had not turned him into a worrier or a ranter at strangers, which is the fate of some lonesome people. He retained his peace of mind and had nothing to prove, but socially he had become frigid. There would be no new chapters. No variations on old themes.

Max felt terrible about all this. The longing he had come to recognize in his father depressed him and left him feeling vaguely guilty. It made him fear for the needs that circumstance and the passing of time visited upon people. It made love and happiness seem to be an accident, the good luck of a pleasant visitation, a surprising distraction from the city, where men and women greet one another in places wholly public, secure, unremarkable.

Max imagined his father in the street. There, what took shape was a golem leaning on a stick, invisible as a monk, while bodies sauntered by, the idols of flesh and virtue. Of poise, presence, elegant virility. To his father's eye these figures must walk naked through the streets, tall as lampposts, thighs like riverbeds, not monstrous—monumental. Parting the crowd.

Still Life with Old-fashioned Dress

The customers new to the café—those who don't know me as Max's father—recognize me as the quotable café regular featured once in the column "Sights About Town," which Ostrovsky has pinned behind glass, beside his menu, in a brushed metal display case out front. The column appeared in a glossy local magazine next to a picture of me shaking Ostrovsky's hand over the bar. We both dressed casually for the event. Since the café boasts no other celebrities—no low class cabinet ministers in for a pint—I was chosen to pose as the grand old man, the Dean of the Café des Westens.

We waited for the photographer all afternoon: a short man, little round glasses; that was all Ostrovsky was told. I took the day off because Hy insisted he needed a friend to shake hands with. That was the kind of shot they wanted. As if he were Babe Ruth and I an adoring fan. Around two o'clock Ostrovsky got fed up and ran up the street to the bank with the deposit from the night before, and I sat watching the store. The place was empty except for one woman in an old-fashioned dress who spent the better

part of the afternoon over a single cup of coffee. Every now and
then she took her lipstick out of her bag to repaint, smacked her
lips and took another sip.

Years back I would have said hello. Not for any reason other
than to pass the afternoon. You used to just talk to people in this
town. Ask them their names, what they did for a living. There was
a time when I stopped to pick people up at bus stops and dropped
them off on the way to work. If you tried that now someone
would call the cops. Or they'd just look right through you, until
you disappeared. Max says it's the same when he picks up a fare.
They sit in the back and adjust their clothes, paint their nails, fiddle with the newspapers they've already read. He says he doesn't
mind the silence. I've tried to get him to quit driving cab. There
was even that poor guy who was killed and locked in the trunk of
his car. I thought that might do it. But the headlines didn't worry
Max a bit. To him it's an honest job. A way to pawn his privilege
in the name of hard labor.

The night I saw him dropping a fare in front of the café, I
should have left him alone. But the car sat out front for such a
long time, I thought maybe he'd come by to say hello. Wishful
thinking. The drunk in the backseat couldn't find his wallet. He
sat with one foot on the pavement, pulling at every pocket. I
wasn't in great shape myself, rumpled and weak in the knees, so
when he lunged from the car, I wasn't exactly ready to set out after
him. Something about the momentum he picked up—or the
drinks he'd had—kept him from straightening out, and he bar-
reled down the block, bent over at the waist, head up and arms
out, as if he were getting ready to fly. He fell once, hard, against a
mound of garbage bags and boxes and then rose again to begin a
second attempt at takeoff. Max and I watched as the drunk taxied
across the avenue and disappeared down an alleyway, still low to
the ground and waving his arms, his suit jacket flared out behind
him.

I should've kept my mouth shut, but it was too rich an opportunity to pass up. I made a big show of sitting in the backseat of the car and sniffing. I told Max the car stank, that I was going to have a word with the skinflint who managed the fleet—tell him my kid doesn't have to drive around in a heap like this. It happens I know the old guy who owns Heart Taxi Service. Litvak started off in town, just off the boat, as a rag and bottle collector. A very fancy operation. So now he's the owner of forty-odd bald-tired Plymouths with little mint-scented evergreens hanging from their rearview mirrors. I know he means well by Max. He's tried to take him under his wing, but in the wrong way. He keeps telling him he could do more with himself, considering that he's a member of the tribe—those are Litvak's words—and has an education. But he rides him too much. I can just hear the old guy saying, *Max, Vy do you come here, anyvay? Monday. Vensday. Friday. You should be out making something of yourself. Building things up.* And I suppose Max gives him the same straight line he's always served me. What should I be building? And old Litvak has two very straightforward answers: Condominiums! *Heizer!* It's the same refrain in every generation: young man, the years are running!

The woman with the lipstick stretched her coffee out to an afternoon's work. She sipped and painted, painted and sipped. In the old days I would have told her about myself. Chances are she had her share of stories to tell. Maybe she would have liked to get in on the photo shoot herself. But when the photographer arrived with his assistant, the activity spooked her, and she packed her things and ran.

When the article about the café appeared a month later, I realized that the assistant had come to take notes because the photo ran next to an interview I was not even aware of having given. Suddenly I had the last word on "The Way It Was":

"I watched Ostrovsky set up. That was in the summer of 1950. He'd disappear into the building, some mornings as early as seven o'clock. I saw him at the window now and then, with his hands behind his apron, and once in a while he'd come out on the sidewalk to help unload a truckload of equipment for the kitchen. I was living by myself in a little firetrap up the street, and from a balcony outside my window, I could see him arranging tables, painting the ceiling with a roller on the end of a long pole. The mornings were bright and calm that summer, with almost nothing going on in the city. While the rest of us played for time, waiting to see where something might open up, whether a friend was going to find you a job, Ostrovsky built himself a little business. I'd known him in high school—a tough type, with all kinds of touchy hang-ups, and you had to be careful around him, careful not to slip into a version of the infectious thick accent he hadn't lost, careful not to imitate his funny lope, careful not to ask him a question about his family he didn't want to answer. He became notorious one autumn for pushing a guy down the school stairs who had innocently asked why he'd left Poland for Canada.

"I thought I'd watch the café before I made my first visit, wait and see just who he was attracting with his Daily Specials. But, as I said, there wasn't much doing in town, and I couldn't hold out for long, avoiding what promised to be easy company, a regular neighborhood crowd.

"The day I went in for the first time, I walked up my side of the street, early. A blonde bearded fellow sat in the window, lifting a coffee cup to his mouth, putting it down, lifting it, taking tiny sips. I pushed open the door and saw five or six other men, all in their fifties and obviously bachelors, with that gray boredom on their faces that comes from too many nights spent in a room alone. One old-timer was crouched over an upright piano set against the far wall. He was playing a slow slightly misfired version of 'Danny Boy,' but even a bit off-key, the song sounded sweet. The fellow sang with an Irish lilt. I couldn't decide if his accent was authentic or staged—and most of the faces in the room looked distinctly East European, so no one was daydreaming of Dublin—but there was a look in their eyes, a trembling about the corners of their mouths that made it seem certain they were all about to break into tears.

"Ostrovsky was nowhere in sight. I remember looking back out at the street where a brand new tan and gold Oldsmobile was pulling up to the curb. The sun slanting through the windshield was so bright the driver disappeared. For a moment the car seemed to drive itself, and the steering wheel jiggled and turned on its own, the helm of a ship that had learned to pilot itself.

"I smiled at a couple of the old guys sitting there, but 'Danny Boy' was too much for them; they were too distracted and heart-broken to respond. So I left them alone and went to the counter, but before I could shout for service, there was a crisp loud noise from the back room—something heavy hitting something hard, and the piano suddenly went silent. The bachelors turned to see what had happened, but no one got up. I watched the swinging doors that led to the kitchen. From the back came a gigantic sneeze that broke the silence. And then another, and the sneezer picked up momentum until his sneezes followed one another as if a machine were making them, shivering and shaking between blasts.

"I stepped over a half-opened crate of ketchup bottles, pushed open the swinging door, and a cloud of fine powder blew out on the draft—it was cinnamon—settling in a rich soft cloud over the room, and Ostrovsky knelt beside the burlap sack he'd dropped, sneezing, looking up at me, as if he were trying to laugh, but also with an expression on his face that begged for help. His sneezes were coming so close together he could barely breathe. Before I could say a word, I drew my own breath of cinnamon and began sneezing myself.

"It was quite a pretty sight, with the sun streaming across the top of the room, riding on the brown cloud, and the two of us yelping at each other, smelling sweet but suffocating. I turned, one hand over my mouth and my nose, and broke for the door. I held it open, expecting Ostrovsky to follow me, but he had grabbed a broom, and wheezing—he was dusted so he looked like a fat gingerbread cookie—he battled the cloud. The bachelors just stared as I crossed the room, leaving cinnamon footsteps on Ostrovsky's new floor."

When the photo shoot was done, and the little man and his assistant had gone, I was an hour late for an appointment. But I couldn't bring myself to rush on such a beautiful afternoon, with the smell in the air of the sun warming the pavement and the sound of the leaves like a woman taking off her coat.

Family Album

A summer afternoon, the leaves are a dark fan the hills hide behind. The sky is the blue of a robin's egg, with a low wreath of cloud. A 1950s city—in the naive style of a child's drawing—with neat-roofed houses, red-brick chimneys, smiling billboards under aluminum shades. The river disappearing, dark and briny beneath the Centre Street Bridge.

Effaced are the web of rails that ran down Eighth, the pith-helmeted and gold-buttoned cop who waved a baton at Model Ts, told Stetsoned men the time from his silver pocket watch, although it was clearly 8:17 by the white replica of a stopwatch that hung over the window of the Alexander Cigar and News Stand. Bicycles tipped against the curbside and against the low lamp-posts. The Rexall Store (CIGARS!) with its ivory display cases, Hotel Royal, The White Lunch, Kolb's, The Lineham Block, Sweet Caporals.

All this has been replaced by the modern pathos for parking

lots. Downtown, looking southwest . . . booming . . . and prosperous. The same square-roofed homes overshadowed by towers sitting satisfied on top of cement parkades. The old granite schools and churches like freak cousins the rich relatives forgot to hide. The Summit Hotel imitates a roll of toilet paper wearing a hat.

The Halloween frost of Max's first autumn in the house. Posing with a friend, they are two white-sheeted clowns with matching orange buckets, half-filled with jujubes, jawbreakers, unpopular baked apples, smashed peanuts and Aero bars. The grass, strangely green under a smokey fall sky. Evening is the color of the sea when it is stirred and stormy but with ribbons of carmine and wisps of rose.

Martin with the staff of his funeral parlor, standing in the shade at the turn in the river behind the old train station. Five awkward men and women: Edith with her eyes on the ground, a young man in an ill-fitting dark suit shuts one eye. Martin, squaring his shoulders, produces a broad smile that shows no teeth.

Thoughts in a Garage

I wait for father out behind the red brick apartment house where we live. I wait and watch as the turning sun draws a line across the grass. I count cats climbing the drainpipe. Overfed monkeys. I watch the old Chinese woman gathering her dandelion harvest. She has her miner's hat on. The little light fixed to the crown is for nightly worm hunts. She gathers her dandelion crop in an empty paint tin with polished silver sides. It is a sacred vessel. She scrapes in the ruts around the shrubbery, along the untrimmed edge of the lawn, up against the walls of the old garage. She has enough for a great vintage barrelful of dandelion wine. Her husband is nowhere to be seen, but he can't be far off. They always move as a pair, she gathering leaves for wine, he, with his gray hair in his eyes, working a tune out of his violin that is one part Vienna, one part Kowloon. I stand just inside the doorway of the garage, watching the dandelion miner and the long grass.

The garage is dark and damp. The heat makes the old boards sag and creak. Shadows smell of oily pine. Firewood piled against one wall is covered in a thick net of cobwebs, and in the upper-most peak of the garage, a bird is skittering, hopping from one beam to another, trying to escape by simply rising.

In this garage, by late summer, there is always an impressive crop of black flies. They cling lazily to the ceiling, too fat and faded to fly. And they fall, one bloated and baked fly after another, abandoning their final roosting place and dropping—tap, tap, tap —onto car roofs. I sit on the dusty firewood and count the rhythm in the fly graveyard.

The ride over to Sara's will be like all the other ones before it. Me, in the passenger seat, the victim of father's predictable questions. His obsessive search for something to keep with him afterward for company, as evidence of things he is sure of before he asks. Every conversation is the same. I refuse to tell him the stories he wants to hear. I bore him. He wants direct narrative, I give him evasions. I ought to have plans, I have none. I tell him that on the day Sara and I first went out I looked out the window from where I lay on the couch and watched the gray sky flatly fallen on the net of branches. I tell him it looked as though it might rain, and we had plans to walk by the river. Awful. How could this happen? How could the summer sky abandon me? I explain that through the dirty window of our apartment it was impossible to tell if rain was falling, dust was blowing, or if the wind moving the trees was rearranging the light falling through the branches. I tell him even more boring things he has no interest in. That there was a rumble outside. An airplane? Street-sweeper? Downpour? No. A big sedan rolling by, squeezing between the cars that lined both sides of the street. An elbow stuck out of the passenger side as if to make the hulking machine a little wider.

Father interrupts, politely, to say that I should know by now how to tell a story. That little details like this are meaningless. Obsessive and a distraction. No one needs to hear which way the light moves. Or how, exactly, the house sounds as it settles into its foundation. And it's a story about a first date, for God's sake. A romance. There are ways to do these things.

So I become a little less discreet, but not much. I might describe our first kiss. Or the feeling of a hand traveling down an arm to clasp another hand. The glisten of lips under a streetlight. There are hundreds of suitable things to tell a man who wants to hear something colorful.

So I admit, we met on a bus.

A bus?

A bus. Father is pleased by this. He settles into his driving and listens, looking straight ahead at the road and smiling. He rolls down the window. His crow's feet open like a lady's fan.

It's true. We met on a City of Calgary bus. One of the oldest in the fleet. It rattled and backfired over potholes. A couple of kids were trying to impress their girlfriends by making fart noises, lifting their bare legs off the vinyl seats fast. Two old women talked loudly in Japanese, yelling above the rattle. And a whole lot of zombies just sat. Zombies holding Eaton's bags and shoe boxes.

Father eyes me again with a look that says, details don't matter, son. The lie of the air. The laughter in the background as some fat lady yells. Tell me a story!

So I give the story some direction. It was her habit, I tell him, of lecturing to anyone willing to listen that led to our meeting.

He enjoys this. Savors it. An hors d'oeuvre. *Whom*, he asks, *did Sara lecture to on a bus?*

Two old men.

This promises a great deal, a point worth pursuing.

I watched her listen to two old men who were arguing about Prague before the war. One remembered it as a fine formal party to which everyone was invited and where everyone was properly treated and well fed. The second man was less anxious to remember a prewar Arcadia. A self-proclaimed realist, he mistrusted

Arcadias. Order then is order now, he said. Different uniforms and another set of forms to fill out, but orders stay the same. In answer to this, the sentimentalist pulled out an article he'd clipped from the newspaper. A long yellowed strip that he held gingerly at top and bottom. He let it hang limp then snapped it. Dust rose. He read, remembering how declarations were once read in town squares, with trumpets, horses' hooves, the leafy trees providing a steady chorus of reply.

"A plea from Czech Punks."

He raised his eyebrows for punctuation.

"They write to President Husak: We would like to inform you of a situation that is getting very serious for us. We are young peo- ple who like punk music as well as the clothing that is associated with it. Because of this we have been unlawfully persecuted by the Plzen PS Security Police for quite a while. We don't provoke them, we might add; it is simply because we wear leather jackets decorated in various ways and have unusual hairstyles. They cut our jackets. Sometimes very expensive ones too. . . ."

The reader's companion interjected here. "Poor things!" Then he caught sight of something interesting on the back side of the clipping and read, *"Magyar SWM 24, 4 eve itt, aktiv, rock zene ked- velo keres magyar fiatalokat. Gabi 698-4569."*

The owner of the clipping cleared his throat, ignoring the inter- ruption, and continued. "They cut our jackets and shave our heads. In addition the PS often beat us for no reason. We must warn you, Mr. President, that such persecutions may, and unfortu- nately do, lead to tragic consequences when we simply cannot bear the pressure and are pushed to the very edge of society."

The bus gave a tremendous jolt. It sounded as though the win- dows might pop out. The reader folded the clipping and slipped it back into his breast pocket.

I am a despised passenger. Father can barely stand the bore- dom. It's hot, the traffic is deadly slow, I am a storyteller without a story. He tries to be patient, fiddles with the rearview mirror.

"Thugs, yes, Imre?" the reader said to the other.

His companion nodded. "Yes. Spoiled rotten. But I must say, I do like those leather jackets on young girls. The way the hair hangs over an upturned collar."

"Imre!" The sentimentalist was disgusted.

"Sorry. Forget I said that. I agree with you. I say send them to do a few months of hard labor. Let them wear something with a few less belts and zippers. It's less fun hauling coal in a smock than hanging around a coffee bar in a costume."

Father waits.

Then Sara interrupted, yelling at the two of them. "Why don't you keep your frustrated theories to yourselves? You're just a couple of impotent bears pontificating about a country you left forty years ago!"

The bus became very quiet except for the two old women yelling in Japanese. It pulled up to a red light, and the windows stopped clattering. The character who read the newspaper clipping was angry. He pulled a manila envelope from a paper bag that he insisted was full of his war medals. It was hard to tell if what he had to show were really medals or just hood ornaments, dainty door knockers and hijacked mezuzahs. He produced another envelope full of bookplates, coats of arms steamed off the inside front covers of volumes in famous Czech libraries. He began to enumerate them, pointing to the mottos that ran beneath each coat of arms and reading them out. *"Pravda Vites,"* he shouted. Truth is Victorious! And no less stirring was the image of the Lion of Bohemia flanked by the Kriván Mountain. The drawings on the plates were little medals themselves, finely etched renderings of trinkets and chains, ribbons, the bridges over the Vltava, the Prague Castle.

Sara listened, waiting till the old gent ran out of things to say, and then asked him, "Have you ever heard of the golem of Prague?"

The loud collector of bookplates frowned. No. His patient partner shook his head in comradely ignorance. Sara informed them that the golem was one of the most famous inhabitants of their city. Possibly the third best known, after King Wenceslaus and Franz Kafka.

And I listened and watched, or better said, watched and listened, as she told them about Rabbi Loew's creature.

Father is worried that I am about to tell him about the golem of Prague. He is utterly disappointed in the way I present this scenario: a woman mastering two old braggarts on a bus—that is what is compelling about the story—and I insist on telling him about the golem of Prague.

The golem of Prague? She told an old monarchist with a bookplate collection about the golem of Prague? About a creature made out of clay who chopped wood and brought water until he went berserk and the rabbi had to turn him back into mud? What the hell kind of story is this?

Father beats the steering wheel with an open palm. It looks for a moment as if he might steer us into oncoming traffic, sacrificing himself and me as well in the name of a story badly told. A story that omits all the proper details, such as what I said to introduce myself to this willful stranger. What the driver did to calm the outbreak stirring at the back of his vehicle. Whether a brawl broke out, the fat ladies flattening the kids, the zombies batting each other with their boxes, Sara somehow rising above the melee like a wise angel?

I should tell him these things, but I don't.

The golem and I drive up Sara's street, he shrunken at the wheel, orange and about to turn back into mud in the late afternoon light. The six o'clock slant of the sun sends yellow and red bars of light through the poplar tree by Sara's window. The blind is drawn in the big bay window, the walkway overgrown on either side by wild crabgrass and a raging late summer crop of dandelions. My golem-father sits imagining the mastery of a pair of almond eyes and an auburn mane. The day's work is only a beginning for him. What passes for business, for labor from nine to five comes to him as easily as breath. It's in the late hours that he begins to struggle. Then his tasks become more troublesome and he shrinks a bit. Lamed. He waits for some fierce mastery to be visited on him. To be told that he must chop wood. Draw water. If only someone would ask something of him and reveal the letters on his forehead, inauspicious, repetitive, hidden letters of an unacceptable code. Letters dictated by need and imaginings whose spell is like the snapping on of a brace, an instrument of torture. This golem is not brought to life to prowl the streets and protect the terrorized and helpless. This one is the helpless who longs for a companion to join him. For this golem the purple sky, pinpricked with ivory, is a perfect cover under which to find a partner. An agreeable creator. Of course, this is all conjecture.

We stop in front of Sara's house. Inside she hides out from business and ambition. She dreams up day jobs that won't last. Free lance contracts that will pay terribly but take up enough time so she can't look for other work. Painting jobs. Research projects on the tea trade or condom use in the Third World. Assignments to go collecting parts for a big motorized contraption that will appear in some friend's independent film for at least a minute. Work like this lets her spend hours scouring thrift shops and junkyards for pipe, light fixtures, bicycles with wheels and without, skates, dolls, exploded handbags, hair dryers, clocks that run in reverse time, typewriter keys, fans, jukebox grills, weather vanes and, of course, old toilets and sinks, the white porcelain bowls like calm centers amidst all the rest of the clutter. Holes softly sucking wind.

Father honks and sets the whole block hopping. Across the

street a pit bull starts to yelp and hurl itself against a wire fence. It has the look of slaughter in its eyes, and I get back inside the car and shut the door, watching to be sure that the dog is trapped in its yard. Three passersby, hermetically sealed into white raincoats and holding briefcases like fifth appendages, give a simultaneous hop of surprise. An invisible band of pigeons directly above them lets go a torrent of shit, croaking and crapping all over the road. The three hermetically sealed men go into a sort of serpentine act to avoid the downpour, looking up in fear and stepping lightly.

Sara's blinds are always drawn, so she sees none of this, but that is how the night begins.

The Essential Oil Business

Max stood with his suitcase beside his father's parking stall. When he was small one of his favorite stunts was to play runaway, to disappear at noon like a thief with stolen goods on his back. He would return hours later and empty his bag of laundry on the carpet in his room. His father greeted him at the door solemnly upon each return, welcomed him, made him dinner and left him on his own to put his things away. Max had done this so many times that he came to be laughed at like the boy in the fable who sets off so many false alarms his unreliability becomes legend. The little boy called cabs and arranged to be met halfway up the block so the neighbors wouldn't see him throw a bag in the backseat. He planned escapes when his father was out of town, feeling ridiculous as he pocketed the door key to prepare himself for the inevitable change of mind.

But this time he was not going in stealth. He would confront his father with the fact of a packed bag. A good piece of work. Martin could drive him with it to the restaurant where they had arranged to meet Sara for dinner, or he could refuse and watch

Max lug the bag up the block to the bus stop. There was justice in this—in making his father respect his departure by giving him a part in it, as the porter who helps a traveler embark on a voyage from which he cannot be called back.

But Martin was late. The garage buzzed and creaked. It stank like an old barrel. The other tenants in the building came home from work, parked their cars, brought their garbage down, collected a broom, a step stool, work gloves. A white-haired woman who lived on Max's floor asked him if he needed some kind of help. He said no. She offered to call him a cab. He told her he was waiting for his father, which elicited an expression Max recognized as the international symbol for pity. She lifted her eyebrows, heaved a sigh and nodded. Then she left.

Max felt embarrassed, as if he were revealing something dirty about himself to his neighbors, standing out in the garage sweating on his expensive case, obviously bought by his father, possibly being used for purposes of abandonment.

The flies buzzed.

The dandelion-mining twosome took their yield and left.

The clouds took their lazy spots in the sky.

Martin was half an hour late. Max was thirsty and wanted a place to sit, so he carried the case across the yard and put it back in the elevator. He dragged it down the hallway to his father's apartment. The white-haired woman was oiling the finish on her front door, turning a rag in big circles on the dark wood, and she could not resist giving Max a second display of pity, taking time out from her work to sigh and nod.

Max had told his father he would meet him out by the garage, but he was sure Martin would look for him in the apartment. He left his bag by the door and used the bathroom. An arrow of sunlight struck the blue and white tiles, a bright spot amidst all the cool shadow. Max sat in the dim room, imagined the arrow was the gnomon of a sundial, the tiles a Peloponnesian floor. All the windows in the apartment were open the three inches allowed by the little brass security contraptions Martin had fixed to the frames. Breezes shuttled across the rug, twittered in the curtains.

In the kitchen Max counted empty liquor bottles. Empties were scattered everywhere—on the windowsill, on the fridgetop, by the sideboards—and some had been put to use as containers for cooking oil, vinegar, rice and peas. Martin got the stock inside with an old tin funnel that sat with its nose upturned on one of the bottles. Dishes filled the sink. An as-good-as-empty ketchup bottle was turned upside down on a plate. Martin was salvaging the last of its contents for their next meal. This was a widower's kitchen. The strange disorder could only be produced by a man who had never learned how to take care of himself. Martin had sold their family home shortly after his wife died, so Max had the opportunity—unique among his friends—to grow up in an apartment block.

An idling engine sang up from the alley below the window. A huge Buick with a dent in the roof was being jockeyed, inch by inch into a too small parking space. And somewhere, from a window indiscernible from all the others in the building, the Bolero erupted, a long slow climax being visited on the neighborhood. It was the laughter in the afternoon of lovers who needed to brag.

Max thought again about taking some of his father's books. These were books he had never wanted to read until he decided to move out. Now they represented lost opportunities. A collection of essays on Confucius, a little green hardback with pencil marks in the margins. Biographies of John A. Macdonald, Winston Churchill, Moshe Dayan. Something by James Michener. A Webster's dictionary. But the thought of opening his bag and then struggling to get it closed again was enough to make him lose interest. He would borrow the books from the library.

His suitcase was a jumble of T-shirts and underwear and jeans with a clock radio and a tennis racket threaded between. On top of this he laid as many of his records as would fit and, as an afterthought, a towel. It was a disorderly bag, but he felt well represented by what was inside.

There was a knock at the door, not much more than a tap, and Max picked up his suitcase expecting to see his father. It was their white-haired neighbor.

"Has your father come back?"

Max was afraid that if he said no he might cause another deadly sympathetic sigh.

"It's business," the woman added quietly, her eyes averted.

"You should call him at work on Monday, Mrs. Stevens."

"I just find it more comfortable talking to him here."

"Whose funeral are you taking care of?"

"Oh, no one's. I'm just laying the groundwork for my own. I don't want my kids to be too burdened."

"I'm sure your children would rather you kept busy with something else, Mrs. Stevens. You're still a very healthy woman."

"No. No. No. They mustn't worry about any of it. I just let them know from time to time if I've changed my plans. Your father has such a nice selection of services. He does his business well."

She nodded and tipped up a bit on her heels to see over Max's shoulder.

"He's really been very comforting to me."

"And a real pleasure for your kids, I bet."

"Pardon me?"

"Nothing."

"It's hard on your father, being alone the way he is. How long has it been?"

"My mother died fifteen years ago."

"I bet he loved her."

"Sure, he did."

"He's a kind man, your father."

"It's nice of you to say so, Mrs. Stevens, but. . . ."

"I'd like to see a picture of her sometime."

"I'd have to go looking for one. Dad put them all away a few years back. He said it just depressed him to have her around, smiling at empty rooms."

Max leaned on the door so it would close a bit.

"Call my dad on Monday, Mrs. Stevens."

"Thank-you, young man."

She backed down the hall, dabbing with her cloth at the river of dust that gathered on the molding. The hall smelled sweet and sour. A mixture of Indian cooking, disinfectant and stale perfume.

The apartment was quiet with just the breeze blowing, jiggling the weights that kept the drapes earthbound against the wall.

Max watched the road for his father's car. A woman pushed a carriage up one sidewalk, an old man on his cane shuffled down the other. If either one turned the wrong way in the sun, bared too many surfaces in the heat, Max was sure they would be overcome, disappear into the wind.

In the building across the alley, every windowpane framed some treasure. A wooden boat, an armless bust of a woman with a bun in her Grecian curls, a huge piece of blue-brown folk art that might have been an oar. A fat man, shirtless, his shoulder stuffed into the window frame, trained his eyes streetward. The angle of his gaze seemed to land at the young mother's feet.

When Max looked back at the street, he saw his father's car pulling away from the curb. It was six o'clock, an hour past their agreed upon time. But Martin hadn't honked or rung the bell. He had come late, checked the garage and left. Now he would go back to the funeral parlor and do a half-hour's work before he went alone to meet Sara, anxious to gripe about how his very busy son couldn't keep a date even when he did almost nothing all day, nothing more than read and loaf with his friends.

Max picked up his bag. It would be a long bus ride to the restaurant where he and Sara and Martin had agreed to eat. He waited for the elevator, eyeing the door behind which Mrs. Stevens was sure to be dusting.

He felt vulnerable out in the street with his bag. He too, like the mother and the old man, might be overcome by the heat. He hunkered down at the bus stop and waited.

Weeks before, Max had seen the basement man in the neighborhood, weaving in and out of doorways on First Street East,
communing with old clapboard, fanning himself by the front windows of failed businesses. Max barely believed in the old man outside of his grandmother's basement. But he said hello to him as he
passed, the bulk of Mr. Thompson parked under an awning in
search of shade. Mr. Thompson growled back at him, told him to
clear off in language befitting the scene. A few weeks later Max
passed him sleeping, rolled out on the grass in Memorial Park
with a flurry of lottery ticket stubs spread around him. One stub
was pressed tightly under a palm against his hip. The sun came out
suddenly over the park, and the basement man stirred on the
grass, kicked his legs and scattered the stubs across the lawn. Max
hurried off. Had the old man won the lottery, or had he just
found something new to collect? Was the sun at his disposal?

A great dry wind was blowing from the west. It put Max's hair
in his eyes over and over again. He straddled his bag protectively
even though he couldn't imagine anything being snatched on this
street in the middle of a bright afternoon. This was a street where
women were still at ease, where no one eyed another out of suspi-
cion, only out of curiosity. An ancient bus, breaking its diesel wind
as it rattled up the street, stopped for him to get on. The other
passengers watched as Max lugged his suitcase to an empty seat.
Then the bus clattered on its way. Nobody made a noise except
the man behind Max who began to sing. He had one arm up on
the back of the seat, the other hanging out the open window, and
he had a sweet voice with a smile in it—there was no need to see
his expression to know it as he sang:

> Would you come
> back to me
> If I had another million dollars?
> You could be Napoleon,
> You could be Caesar
> But to be somebody in Calgary

You've got to go
to Speedy Muffler King.
It's this year's style
Get it now
before it goes out of style.
Don't throw it away
till next year,
This year they had a style
Next year
They'll have a garbage bag.
At the banana store there's
No cherries.
Ya da da
da da da da
Dee dee dee
dee dee dee dee
And try to smile
once in a while
Oh, would you come back to me
If I had
another million dollars?

Max turned and smiled at the face that sang nonsense so sweet-ly, but the man ignored him, held his pose as if he were alone and switched to a hum.

Max and Martin had agreed to meet at a restaurant that was hidden away in the lobby of a hotel. In front of the hotel, white-hatted overdressed men and women were getting off a Grey-hound. The marquee above the parking lot announced: WELCOME —DARE TO BE DIFFERENT! The white-hatted crowd wore but-tons with the same slogan on them, which Max assumed was an inside joke. The entire busload of men and women looked per-fectly alike, their shoes well shined, their raincoats well pressed and folded neatly over one arm, all carrying a copy of the local tabloid as if it were their passport to the surrounding territory.

The final edition displayed a photograph of the newly proclaimed Miss Canada on the front page. Big white block letters cried, SHE'S THE QUEEN!

The doorman opened the big glass door for Max and tipped his cap. Max headed for a side door where he had to let himself in. He put the bag down as a doorstop, circled around it and pulled it inside after him. Back out at the curb, a second doorman was loading a pile of identical gray Samsonite bags onto a cart.

Sara sat in an overstuffed tulip-shaped chair in the center of the lobby. Max limped up to her with his bag on his heel.

"I have left," he said.

"I can see that."

"You don't sound convinced."

"You've left before, Max."

"But this time I packed properly."

"Will the bag eat dinner with us?"

"No." Max had not considered this. He did not want the bag as a dinner guest. It would rebuke him. His father would include it in every turn of the conversation.

"I'll check it at the desk."

Max surrendered his bag—a badge of newfound independence —and sat beside Sara in a chair that matched hers. It was not easy to sit up straight in this kind of furniture. The upholstery accepted hips like a gift, took them down into folds deep as seams in a land-scape. Max and Sara were held captive, separated from each other by a little cocktail table. The muzak provided the perfect score for their predicament: strings bewailing their dusty shoes, vibes ringing like secret alarms to alert the proper authorities that these two loiterers had no particular business in the hotel.

Max and Sara said nothing, only acknowledged each other with sidelong glances as if they were spies, incognito, but too dumb to move from the first quiet place they found to sit.

The hotel was a kind of temple. One with indiscriminate rules where money changers and whores did miraculous business. The walls were covered with rich wood paneling, the floors inlaid with sparkling travertine. Pairs of big fake Louis Quatorze mirrors hung opposite each other down the length of the lobby so the space replicated itself into a hundred minuscule eternities. Lamps introduced a Polynesian nightclub theme, shades of the opium den. Mock Ming dynasty jugs collected dust.

A woman with a well-taped hockey stick—possibly an Olympian at summer training camp—shimmered by all in white leather, the fat black blade of her stick upturned. The crowd of look-alike white-hatted men and women, still daring to be different, paraded on the thick rugs to the sound of country and western music. The sacred wail of pedal steel and saw floated down from invisible ceiling speakers. And the comers and goers were anointed, though many were unaware; they were made fragrant by a scent that came and went, was faint and then rose to a nauseating height.

"A splash of tuberose and mecca balsam." A voice spoke above the muzak. "Esprits de rose, jasmine, cassia, essence of musk and ambergris." This chant came from a stall at one side of the lobby.

The first voice was interrupted by a shriller one.

"Bouquet d'amour?" It was the Olympian in leather who reached after the vial and held it to her nose, sniffing. "No man-made scent is as nice."

"We have the same scent in cassiolettes for the drawer," returned the first voice. "These will also keep moths away, madam."

Max and Sara watched a crowd gather around the lady's display of tiny bottles. Held tightly in the chairs' grip, their eyes wide like children's eyes, amazed, their mouths open against their will. They sunk deeper into the cushions, their thoughts awash in scent and the names of scent and in the voice of the woman who was such a compelling priestess of scent. She stood behind the makeshift counter erected by the door of her store and made solicitous faces, nodded in agreement when customers praised her wares. She had high arching eyebrows and a massive forehead from which her hair was pulled fiercely back.

"The splash of myrtle, rose, ylang-ylang," she said to the Olympian who sniffed another ampule and sneezed.

Sara overcame her distraction long enough to ply Max with information. Ylang-ylang, an aromatic tree native to the Philippines, having fragrant drooping flowers that yield a volatile oil. Myrtle, anciently held sacred to Venus and used as an emblem of love.

Sara brought forth a litany Max would never remember no matter how hard he tried. Tolu, verbena, neroli—derived from the flowers of the orange tree—and as the exotic catalogue dragged on like a hypnotist's chant, there appeared to Max in the interstices of these ingredients, in the rhythm of Sara's breath, which was quick but clear, a reflection of himself, an image repeated again and again and receding in an endless chain that could be mounted like a vanishing stairway, each image identical but smaller than the one before it. He saw his father coming toward him down a rich rug, one hand ahead of him, the other deep in his pocket. And his father came forward and passed by him, came forward and passed, in an eternal return that was dizzying. A season without end.

His arms and belly light as feathers, Max felt he played no part in the rush of activity around him, as if he hovered up near the ceiling and heard the gathering crowd on the carpet from far away.

Ambergris, musk, Sara continued, Hungary water—believed to have miraculous qualities—and in the harmony of these scents, for scent has, Sara said, harmony and discord like music—in the harmony of these scents the ladder of receding images altered, closed up like an accordion into a single frame in which a young man Max's age sat in a waiting room, surrounded by other young men and women. The men wore flowing silk ties and loose gabardine jackets. The women all wore skirts, blouses neatly tucked around the thinnest waists. Their hair was the color of baked clay. They were dressed in blue, carmine and emerald, pinned like butterflies against the backs of couches, their eyes trained aimlessly into cor ners and out of windows. The young man—whom Max recognized as himself—held a newspaper folded once between each thumb and forefinger. Neither his eyes nor the newspaper moved, as if he read the same word over and over again.

A voice that sounded behind a wall listed the ingredients for a bizarre recipe, and it became clear that the pinned forms and aimless eyes were made so by a tense attendance to this voice.

"Essence of bergamot oil," it said. It was a woman's voice. Very firm and clipped. There was never a hesitation between words. "Two and a half drachms. Oil of lavender, one drachm. Aromatic and glacial vinegar, one-half drachm each. Essence of musk, three fluid ounces. Mix, with agitation, as before. Very fine."

The waiting room was unnervingly quiet when the voice stopped. The young figures were rapt with anticipation and threatened to topple, to come unpinned. They paid no attention to the wonderful views that fell away on either side of the room: a river off toward the horizon in the west, a tin-roof town to the east, surrounded by a swirl of brush and wind.

The voice began again. This time a man's voice was also heard in response to each ingredient the woman named.

"Esprit de jasmine, one pint."

"Uh."

"Spirit of hyacinth and tincture of styrax, half a pint each."

"Mm, yes." The answering voice was tentative and halfhearted, as if the man taking part in the process did not trust himself with the work.

"Spirit of star-anise and tincture of tolu, two fluid ounces."

"Hmm."

"Essence of vanilla and ambergris, one-half drachm."

There was a yelp. "Yud Lamed!"

"What? What have I done?"

"Don't shake. It must digest before it is shaken. Oh, Yehudah Leib. A schlimazel such as you the world has never seen!"

The men and women in the waiting room straightened themselves up as if they hadn't been listening, adjusted ties, pulled at skirts when a stocky gray-haired man burst through a door toward them, buttoning his smoking jacket as he came. "The chores are done," he said, one eye checking the alignment of his buttons. "My wife only employs me in the early stages. The more delicate steps she carries out by herself. It is this that saves her Essential Oils shop from bankruptcy, she says. So which one of you is next? This lady standing by the window?"

The woman turned, made to come forward, but she retreated as he looked past her at another woman who stared up from where she sat.

Yehudah Leib was a very elegant looking man with soft disdainful eyes, almost oriental, half-closed. He affected the dress of an Asian gentleman, wearing a brocaded vest, a tall colorful cap and knee britches that were purple and green.

"Or the young lady in the pink collar. Ah, your face is a gathering of shadows. A wonderful Semitic face. Full of storm clouds and darkening years."

The young people in the room stirred. Yehudah Leib looked past this woman, and she became fixed again, caught in the pillows where she sat.

"No. I recognize my next visitor." For the first time the newspaper stirred in the hands of the green-suited young man. His face turned pale. Color drained out of him till he looked like a plaster cast, overdressed. He stuttered.

"It, it, it's. . . ."

"It's a great pleasure," the older man prompted.

"It's a g–great p–pleasure for me, Herr professor, sir," and he lost his breath again, let out a sound like a deflating tire.

"I know, I know. To be here and to have the opportunity for me to read your work and offer my judgment, kind or harsh. Harsh, even from me would suit you, would it not?"

The young man nodded.

"Harsh words from the heights are more meaningful than a joy ous sound. Levity being unheard of in matters of earnest judgment."

The young man wagged his head in agreement and repeated the other man's name as if it were part of a prayer. The older led the younger into a small anteroom, shut the door behind them so the other figures, pinned yet open-eared, vanished.

The little study was lined with books, tapestries, tasseled lamps. Footstools and armchairs were so numerous and pressed so tightly together that a visitor did better to walk on a platform of upholstery than tread on the floor.

"Come a little closer, friend."

The young man battered his shins on all the loose pieces of furniture, mumbled and coughed as he tried to communicate his predicament.

"Where to sit? I know. I know. Just put your feet up anywhere, young man. And let me see your manuscript before I take down another to read. There is a work over here," he went hopping from seat to seat toward the book-lined wall, "a friend sent over a month ago. . . ." Then he came hopping back. "Your work. Your work. Give it here, young man. Terrible how scared you all are. Youth afraid. With our youth afraid nothing will get done. I wonder if we parents make you so. I wonder if there is something in my stories that makes you fear me." He put the young man's manuscript into his vest pocket and forgot it there. "But I'm glad you came. Take the first train home. You know the roads around this neighborhood are not reliable."

And the Great Man led his visitor back to the waiting room, left him in the pillows where he found him and went back toward his study, leading the lady with the marvelous Semitic face, who was stuttering, the old man replying, "I know. I know. To be here and to have the opportunity for me to read your work and offer my judgment, kind or harsh. Harsh, even from me would suit you, would it not?"

The young man in his pillows, the way to the train forgotten, returned to his newspaper. The voice of a self-assured sales lady explained from behind the wall, "Yes, we have cassiolettes to keep a drawer fresh. These will also ward off moths, madam. Moths in summer will eat your sweaters whole. Fly away with them in their belly like big buzzing moons."

The list of unheard of extracts of tree bark and fruit rind went on and on. Even the measurements were foreign—the ephahs and drachms of failed civilizations. But the attraction held. There was no less love of scent because its units of measure were antique.

Myrtle, mecca balsam. Tuberose—Sara recited—a bulbous plant of the agave family, cultivated for its spike of creamy white lilylike flower. Max watched himself struggle in the mirror that hung on the wall beside them. The pillows pinched his bottom. As he got up, Martin came through the lobby doors, tipping the doorman, who in turn tipped his cap. Martin's hair was combed neatly where it was thinning, his short sleeves fluttered a bit, as if a breeze followed him, and his pants were worn in the seat, a pair his wife would never have let him leave the house in.

"Let's eat," Martin said. "Max, I'm sorry I missed you. Were you at the apartment?"

As they walked toward the restaurant, Sara fell behind and whispered, "What about your bag?"

Max was straight-faced. "What bag?"

Dinner Talk

So they sat after dinner and filled their dessert cups with watermelon seeds—the soft ping, ping, ping of fruity fireworks sounding in the empty restaurant. The waiter had nothing else to do so he doted on them, barely concealing his lust for a big tip as he demurely poured coffee and removed the empty plates. He recognized Martin as a businessman—possibly an owner of duplexes—as someone who carried a variety of bills, fewer small ones than large. Martin concentrated all his attention on picking at his teeth with a toothpick. He squeaked with his tongue against each tooth and then moved on to the next.

He would hear nothing more until he wanted to. Max and Sara might have plotted a murder over dessert without him knowing, dropping the topic only when his eyes focused again.

Watermelon seeds piled up in little pyramids.

Martin put down the toothpick when it became bloody, the empire of his gums breached.

"So who is this Bruno? And why is he a better housemate than I am?"

"You're not comparable, dad. I'm not moving out because of you. It's because of me."

Martin put the bloody toothpick between his two front teeth. "But we've done so well together this summer. Give me one good reason why you think you shouldn't live at home."

"One would be that you two fight all the time." Sara put her hand on top of Martin's to soften her remark. "And you never stop telling him how to live, Martin. You're turning him into your little eunuch."

"I don't tell him how to live. Max can tell me anything, and I don't interfere."

"So tell him about Bruno, Max."

Martin developed a very pained expression. Max explained that he didn't know Bruno very well and that he suspected he might like him if he did, but he was unreachable and strange, something to do with dead parents and many crises in his young life. He was an artist or at least a pretender. He did very little work and talked a lot. He paraded all the proper slogans of the left, of anti-racism, of anarchy.

Martin studied the pile of watermelon seeds in front of him.

There was no chance of becoming close to Bruno, Max explained, because there could be no common ground with him. His sexuality was suspect because he had none. His friends were acid dealers, pound officers, skateboard freaks and writers with no corpus. Bruno made films that never appeared anywhere but on the cracked walls of the house he lived in. He plowed up the back-yard and tried to plant sunflowers, but the hopeless midget stalks blew away like everything else had that summer. He threw great parties, the news of which always attracted hundreds of uninvited guests. He was miserably outcast and strangely attractive.

"My new roommate."

Martin produced a new toothpick. "People like that will do anything. They've got nothing to lose. This sounds like a very bad idea, son."

"Dad, you can't resort to that. Calling me son won't settle this."

"So I'm alone then, abandoned." Martin said these words slowly and very clearly, as if they demanded counting.

"He's not abandoning you, Martin. It's just a new direction."

But Martin continued to talk slowly, like a sentenced man. "I have nothing now, Max. Just time and nothing to do with it. Do you think you and Sara will come by now and then for dinner?"

There were no seeds left to spit, and the lusty-eyed waiter was nowhere in sight. The restaurant was empty, ugly, the sky orange and violet behind glass.

Max told Martin what he had packed, what he had left in his room. Told him how he'd waited in the garage, and Martin grew angrier at the thought of his neighbors gossiping about Max and his packed bag.

"We agreed on five o'clock, dad. You could've been on time."

"We agreed on six."

"Five."

"Sara?"

It was Sara who raised the subject of the party. "We were going to ask you to come along, Martin. Would you like to go?" Her suggestion sounded very warm and forgiving next to Martin's accusations and Max's recriminations. Somehow it ruined the argument. "Let's take your father to meet Bruno. He can see the house, take stock of the guests. Maybe that will clear things up."

Neither Max nor Martin spoke as they followed Sara around the empty tables and out onto the street where a neat row of flags flapped, and the leaves on the few trees that endured in their sidewalk boxes showed their indifferent faces and laughed, rustling.

On their way to the car, the streetlights flashed on, still needless in the evening glow. Dark flocks of birds followed one-way streets south.

Overheard at a Party

The house, as they say, kissed the ass of Mount Royal. It did not have the pedigree of some houses further up the hill toward Cabot and Wolfe and all the other streets with heroic names, but it had a colorful history nonetheless. It was built at the turn of the century for the Reverend M. Elisha Brown and his wife, but when the lady died—of suspicious cause, as the story goes—it was sold to a group of pioneering philanthropists who had decided they wanted to found a convent. This act, they thought, was righteous and philanthropic to the proper degree to ensure them a place on the honor roll and get their names off the tax rolls. The man who oversaw Calgary's little Catholic community was contacted—his diocese reached as far south as Medicine Hat—and the rich men's spokesman put forward his colleagues' wish to buy the Brown house, to outfit it properly—their proposal included a big fountain out back with a life-size statue of Mary—and to prepare there a holy place for honest souls to devote their lives to the celebration of the cross.

Max pointed to the white head of Mary, all spattered with

pigeon shit, as they pulled up in front of the house. She stood by
the fence at the edge of the backyard, head bowed in supplication
to all who bothered to look, her fountain dry and scaly, the little
brick retaining wall that circled her cracked and jumbled. One end
of a volleyball net was tied to the statue's slender neck. The other
end was hidden behind the house.

A big poplar pressed itself against one side of the house, an oak
against the other, scratching at the windows, trying to get inside
and lift the whole mess of brick and trim off the ground to give it
a shake. The driveway was matted with pine cones and poplar
spoor of fluff and seed. The grass was thin and high. White-
topped dandelions lifted their heads above the gone-to-seed
shoots. All the storm doors swung loose, and the old storm windows were broken. Through the shattered panes around the
veranda, you could see the floorboards strewn with telephone wire,
plumbing fixtures, skateboard wheels. There was a sandy pit
against one wall where someone had torn out a lilac bush. The old
fir trees had gone sickly black, their needles carpeting the ground,
trunks wild as totems, the design of better years. In the peak of
the eaves, crowning all this disrepair, hung a fat gray wasp's nest,
its underside open and swirling.

The house looked to Martin like a place that might have shel-
tered generations of mass murderers.

Max took his father's arm and led him up the driveway, pairs of
old white granite slabs with little jungles of weed springing up
between them. The yard was a wasteland of shattered stonework,
yard-high thistles and a scattering of wild roses and skeletal lilac
bushes that remained from a time when the land was worked by
more careful owners. The same owners who had lovingly white-
washed Mary and filled her fountain with holy hose water. Two
magpies chased a squirrel across the lawn.

Twenty broad steps led up to the front door, which was oak,
rounded at the top under a granite archway. A balcony hung out
above the doorway, and a pair of French doors had been thrown

open so that white curtains clung to the outside of the house. Young people hung over the wooden guardrail and grabbed at a flag that flapped just beyond their reach.

Max squeezed Martin's arm. "I love this place, dad."

Martin scuffed a toe on the cracked steps. "That's good, son," and bending close to Max's ear, he whispered, "Who's the creep on the stairs?"

"That's Bruno."

Bruno balanced a sheaf of paper on one knee and sketched with a fountain pen, dipping it in a jar of ink that sat beside him on the step. He looked more like a gargoyle than any human form Martin had ever seen, with his legs crossed, a hand wrapped around one knee, his profile turned downward and slightly cocked as he judged whatever it was that he was drawing. When Bruno saw them he stood and waved. He was dressed like a banker from the thirties, or some even more distant era. He wore a charcoal jacket and pants with a fuzzy gray pinstripe, a dark shirt and a loosely knotted white tie. A handkerchief peeked out of his pocket. His pants had cuffs. Martin imagined these must be full of sand and dried leaves. The only thing Bruno wore that didn't match the rest of his outfit was a pair of black house slippers, which peeked out from under his trousers. His hair was cut short—even shorter than Martin's—and was greased back on a severe southwesterly angle. A barely noticeable wave of graying hair glinted on one side of his part.

Bruno smiled, his hand out. "I'm glad you're early, Max. And you brought Sara and your father. Glad to meet you, Mr. Binder."

Martin was staring at the figure before him as if he were trying to see out the back of its head. Sara squeezed Max's hand, and Max gave his father a nudge.

"I'm pleased to meet you, Bruno. So you're the landlord."

"No, no. I just pay the rent. Max is going to split it with me. I've had a few dry months lately."

Martin felt like saying he could certainly see that, that anyone who dressed like a vampire in August was liable to have dry months. Then he considered that Bruno looked very comfortable for a man wearing a hundred-year-old wool suit in August and that a man would have to have the metabolism of a carp not to be slathered in sweat.

Sara started up the steps, and Max followed. When she pushed open the door, music escaped, a slow sludge of sound, like a recording of a factory amplified and set to a syncopated drum beat.

Bruno led Martin to the bar, poured him a drink and the two turned to face the room. The windows at the back of the big room were opened wide, and the evening light fell in bright spots on the blonde wood walls. The birds outside sounded very happy. Martin picked his way through the crowd with Bruno on his elbow and stood where the light was strongest, his knee resting on the sill. The backyard was a half-acre of tilled mud. A flowering ash towered over Mary and her little fountain. Back by the fence was a stand of spent lilacs. In the center of the muddy yard was a plaster birdbath on a pedestal.

"I tried to plant sunflowers out there this summer. I figured I'd roast and salt a whole truckload and sell them to cover the rent. But I couldn't get enough water through the hose to get everything growing. The government's after me for the $2000 start-up loan they gave me. What do you think, Martin? Has it rained once since April?"

"Not that I can remember. There was that one shower in June."

"It was sad to watch my little sprouts shrivel up. Now I know how farmers feel when the whole field blows away."

"I guess you can try again next year."

"Nope. The landlord's got an asphalt company coming next week to pave the whole thing over."

Martin looked at the mud and calculated the cost. "Is that the best thing he can think of to do with his money?"

"It's a long story. Do you need another drink?"

Martin shook his head, still calculating the cost of tar per square foot of yard.

"This house used to be a convent. The sisters ate in this room. Their supper table was at least twenty feet long. I moved in the day they took it out. The movers chopped it up and took it home for firewood. But I bet the wood was too hard to burn. My bedroom, I understand, was a prayer chapel."

Martin laughed, looked around at the people in the room and tried to imagine one of them praying. The crowd was made up of all types. Couples, oddballs nursing a drink alone in corners. Two thin blondes were entwined on a love seat. Martin was unsure if they were of the same sex, and if so, which. They kissed, barely touching each other's lips, posing, Martin thought, as some kind of priests of love.

"The sisters had a lot of stuff we didn't need anymore. Rosaries on every doorpost. Gardening equipment. There was a garage full of whitewash for Mary. The strangest relic was a little mock graveyard they'd set up out back. Four neat rows of five black crosses each to remind them of the sisters who had predeceased them. They stuck the metal spikes in very deep so the wind wouldn't take them. I would have left them out there. I could have used them to hold up my sunflowers. And they made a good croquet patch. But the landlord wanted them out. They bugged him. He would come over for the rent or to fix something, and he'd always end up standing out back, shaking his head, reading the little white-painted words, pronouncing Latin badly, one syllable at a time. *Re–qui–es–cat Pa–ce*. I'd follow him out there, and he'd say, Would you look at this, Bruno. What in the hell is all this? Every month he'd ask me the same thing. Are these broads buried here or what? And I'd tell him no, Mr. Kruczinski, I think it's a memorial. Then he'd read and reread the names on each marker. Sister Mary Benigna, died October 28, 1936. Sister Mary Anastasia, dead the 15th of March, 1938. Sister Mary Blandina, died September 11, 1939. He was always asking me, What the hell kind of a name is

Blandina? He just couldn't understand how a nun could have a name like Blandina. One day he drove his pickup around back, tied a rope to it and pulled out those crosses one by one. They were in tight though. It was like pulling teeth. He was so pleased when he had them piled up in the back of his truck. He told me he was going to melt them all down and make crowbars out of them. I don't think that business ever got off the ground."

"Sort of like your sunflower project."

"I suppose. But once the crosses were out, their neat little holes were left behind. Twenty neat dimples in the lawn. And this was when I realized that Mr. Kruczinski was obsessed. He was sure those holes were getting deeper every month. He'd come over and watch them, and he swore they were getting deeper. He dumped a yard of loam out back and spread it around, but he said he could still see those holes under the new earth. So he had the yard rototilled, turned like a farmer's field. That's when I tried my sunflower scheme. And Kruczinski insisted my flowers died for untoward reasons. That's the word he used. Untoward. He got this funny look in his eye and smiled. Just remember, Bruno, he'd say, sticking a finger in my ribs, there's nothing blacker than a dead nun's heart." Bruno looked out at the yard. "Now the asphalt's coming. I figure we can tear down the caraganas and rent parking spots."

One fat cloud was moving back and forth over the low orange sun. A silver balloon on a string bounced along the furrows of mud in the backyard.

Sara stood across the room. She talked to a man with a beard. Martin watched her raise her glass to drink. She rested a fist on her hip and nodded at what the beard said. In the slanting sun, with light bouncing off the brown wood, Martin could see the tiny bubbles burst on the surface of her drink. Sara looked up and noticed Martin watching her. He pointed at her glass, raised his eyebrows. She nodded and left the beard alone to sip his drink.

Bruno had vanished.

In the intervening moments, Martin wanted to stand alone, to do the thing that on every other day, hour to hour, was the very exercise that tired him out. He wanted, just for the moment until Sara returned with two drinks—little bubbles breaking on their surface—to remain alone. Solitary like a piece of furniture. But a couple was approaching on his left, each distinctly of a different sex than the other but both of exactly the same shape: bathtub-oval, long, wide and solid. The man wore a T-shirt that read FUCK YOU GWEN! The woman wore one that read FUCK YOU BOB!

Martin offered his hand, as much to keep the two of them at a distance as to greet them. "I'll bet you're Bob," he said as he shook the man's hand.

Bob half-grabbed, half-slapped Martin's open palm. "Hey there, buddy. Me and Gwen looked over and we saw you all alone over here, and Gwen said to me, 'Now Bob, doesn't that gentleman look uncomfortable standing all alone over there,' and I thought you did, so here we are to keep you company."

"That's nice of you folks." Martin swallowed the last of his drink and set the glass on the windowsill. "But a friend is just getting me a drink. And it's been a bad day. I'm really not the best guy to keep company with."

This disclaimer only heightened Bob and Gwen's enthusiasm. "We'll pick you up," Bob insisted. "We think of it as our hobby." Bob explained that he and his wife were indirectly involved in the entertainment business, that they had devoted their adult years to other people's pleasure.

The three of them stood grinning and nodding in silence, practicing the awkward pleasantries that prevail when conversation fails.

"So what's brought you here tonight?" Bob opened his eyes wide like a marlin out of water.

"My son's moving in here with Bruno."

Bob and Gwen oohed and ahed with an enthusiasm that Martin thought was altogether too excessive to be sincere.

"What brings you two here tonight?"

"Bruno was a good friend of our Ted."

"Ted?"

"Oh, our son, Ted. He called himself Lincoln on stage. But we thought everyone in town knew him as Ted."

"Ted."

"Yes, Ted. He was a country and western singer. A folk poet, they used to call him in the reviews in the *Herald.*"

"Gwen, why don't you go tell Bruno to put on one of Ted's demos. I'm sure he's got a tape."

Gwen went off to arrange this, and Bob and Martin looked out at the mud. The industrial noise that had been posing as background music stopped, and the sound of a crowded tavern—glasses tinkling, murmuring voices—filled the room. Bob put a hand on Martin's shoulder and turned him away from the window, as if to ensure he heard the music. A guitar rhythm began that mimicked the sound of a rolling locomotive. Boom–ba–doom–ba, boom–ba–doom–ba. Gwen returned to Bob's side, and they looked at each other with broad smiles. They listened, chins raised, rapt.

Martin concentrated on the music, its steamrolling country groove and the vocalist's deep throaty twang, which reminded him of a first-class auctioneer. The song had one four-line verse that was repeated like a Nashville mantra, said again and again until the words vanished into their own regularity and rhythm:

> Singin', hey Jack
> Don't give me no flack.
> Where the hell is
> My pink Cadillac?

"Ted always did want a pink Cadillac." Gwen looked out the window, and Bob put a hand on her shoulder. Martin felt like an intruder—he was about to excuse himself when Gwen turned away from the window and gave him a solemn look that forecast tears. "It's just that he's been gone such a short time and we're still not used to it."

"He was our favorite," Bob nodded. They looked like a pair of sad-eyed clowns with their joke T-shirts stretched wide around their midriffs.

Martin felt a very great need for another drink. He thought of Sara waylaid by someone in the kitchen, his drink warming in her hand. He was about to tell Bob and Gwen that he understood how they felt because he had been without his wife for fifteen years now and still felt as though she was in another corner of the room, about to join him. There was no end to that strange kind of hope as far as he could tell. But the thought of discussing this depressed him, and he went back to his daydream of the drink that hadn't arrived.

"His career was just about to take off when he died." It was Bob's turn to stare wistfully at the backyard. "We always knew he had a problem with junk. He kept a drawer full of it in his old room at the house. He was sure no one would ever guess he kept a stash there. And the stuff seemed to keep him level. It got him through the bare times." Bob shook his head slowly in time with the music. "He just needed a bit more time. Remember that last show, Gwen?"

Sara appeared with two drinks, and Martin released a loud sigh. He and Sara stood quietly, a bit overwhelmed, as Bob and Gwen reminisced about the songs Ted played at his last show. The originals, the covers, the way the band sounded in the tiny beer hall. Then the proud parents began a duet of their favorite tune, clapping and singing above the sound of their son's recorded voice:

> Workin' in a coal mine,
> Goin' down, down, down,
> Workin' in a coal mine,
> Hhew
> I'd like to sit down.

Half the room turned to see where the chorus was coming from, and Martin interrupted before they could begin another round.

"You two really loved your son."

"Of course we did." Gwen looked irritated.

Sara gave the glass in Martin's hand a push, signaling that he should shut up and drink. "And you were behind him in his career."

"Sure. Gwen and I helped whenever we could. We even helped him pick his stage name. We went through a bunch before he settled." This was a cue for Gwen to chime in, "Barroom Ned." The two of them then took turns listing the discarded pseudonyms.

"Long Tall Ed."

"Jelly Mountain Red."

"Big Daddy Ted."

"Mississippi Fred. It was at one of our barbecues that he made up his mind. Bob was cooking burgers, I'd made up some salad and Ted had his guitar. He sat on the hood of somebody's Ford and sang with the smoke and chicory blowing around him. The big leafy tree was rustling in the wind. And that's when it occurred to him: Lincoln Ford. Just turned around the name on a Ford Lincoln."

Bob and Gwen sighed.

Martin was afraid he might begin to rant about dead loved ones. About sons who left their parents behind, who changed their names on a moment's notice. But his head was a rush of drinker's thoughts that kept his mouth shut. The shopping list he had not shopped for. The things he wanted to ask Sara. His son's incomprehensibility. The strangeness of this old convent house. It wasn't unwelcoming, but there was something unreadable about it, as if it were built on principles he was unfamiliar with. Drinking made everything take on a familiar tone and pace, but this didn't help him cope with the curiosities that surrounded him. He overheard all kinds of inanities as he stood by Sara's elbow, no longer listening to Bob and Gwen's lament. Sara was saying something about Murphy beds. She wondered whether anyone could make Murphy beds or only the descendants of Murphy. He was certain he overheard someone behind him say, "There's a lot of dentists in here tonight." And a dissertation was being given to his left on the ways one could pun on the word sultana. "It means," the disembodied voice announced, "the wife, mother, sister or daughter of a sultan, or a small white seedless grape used for making raisins." Martin imagined himself to be a driver passing through all this, each curiosity like a sign on the roadside that passed too quickly. He remembered a bird he had seen once, hanging on a bent rush beside the highway to Banff. He'd described it to friends who knew something about birds—it was black with a red spot on each wing—but no one had ever been able to name it for him.

Martin excused himself, touching Sara on the elbow as he left.

On the Stairs

Martin pushed through the crowd in the front hall. He did not want to hear another half-finished conversation. On the steps he nearly tripped over Bruno, who was still crouched there like an overdressed gargoyle. They eyed each other in the purple dusk.

"Mr. Binder."

"Bruno, I'm off. If I get involved in one more crackpot conversation I may not be responsible for what I say."

"Are you and Max at it again?"

Martin crept down the side of the steps clear of Bruno and his artifacts. "Your friends Bob and Gwen were trying to cast me in their personal Spaghetti Western."

Bruno came down three steps and offered Martin a hand, a dark-clad doorman handing his guest down to a waiting car. "But they have a kind of charm, don't they? They're as honest as the day, Martin. Can I call you Martin?"

"Sure, Bruno." Martin felt uncertain of what was underfoot and let Bruno lead him.

"They're friends of mine. I made a documentary about their

son." Bruno led Martin across the darkened driveway to a stone bench. "A document of Ted's rare talent. He was really ignored by the industry. It was a tragedy. I got quite attached to the dead man myself. I've still got his guitar and his boots up in my bedroom."

Martin watched a big bank of cloud in the eastern sky that carried a reflection of the city's lights. The moon was setting into the shine and silver that surrounded it. Bruno acted as if all this were the backdrop for his own private stage. He described scenes from Bob and Gwen's daily routine: Bob's black socks and shoes sunning themselves on the windowsill, Gwen swishing water around in her teapot, wieners sweating in a pan, someone's recollection of the way Ted whistled "Alexander's Ragtime Band." Martin's reaction to all this was to ask himself over and over, *Where was Max, where was that kid?* What was he doing moving into a house presided over by a vampire who models antique clothes? It looked to Martin like the beginning of the end. Like the gathering up of a good young man into a wasted life, into a little coterie of poseurs who were too green to realize what kind of future was in store for them. He imagined one disastrous outcome after another.

Martin realized he was alone. Bruno's endless flapping and narrating had stopped without him noticing. The bench was uncomfortable. It was too dark to read the time on his watch. But the fuzzy pinstripe quickly reappeared. Bruno trotted down the stairs and handed Martin a drink—a straight scotch, poured into the type of water glass favored at the Café des Westens.

"Funny thing at this house, Bruno. Everyone's busy getting me a drink."

"That's because you look so uncomfortable."

As Martin got drunker he got quieter, a deeper listener to his own thoughts. Bruno mistook Martin's silence for attentiveness and went on rifling his catalogue of tales about Bob and Gwen. Bruno was the kind of carny-style operator who overwhelmed Martin at the best of times. He was an actor, adept at accents, at

mimicking his friends, at telling loud, long and detailed epics with
no conclusive ending. He sounded like Hank Williams on speed,
twangy and shrill, mumbling insistently like a fly caught between
two panes of glass. "Ted was," Bruno intoned, the odd archaism
creeping into his false Texas drawl, "a gentleman. The last man of
conscience on Eighth Avenue. I will tell you, he used to say, I will
tell you, that there is nothing in this city I crave. Not the houses,
and god knows there's plenty of them, not the girls, their fine
smell in summertime, not even the view from the foothills. Maybe
a pink Caddy, maybe. And I say maybe because a white one would
do just fine. But nothing more. Not all the crap that men today
think is the be-all and end-all. I see these guys, just boys in expensive pants with hair cuts that don't fit 'em quite right. They figure
the highest form of life is to sleep in, to lie in an air-conditioned
spot of sunlight with their lady, giving the cat a poke every now
and then."

Martin finished his drink. Bruno's ramblings only helped to fuel
the dread and disappointment he felt over Max's plans. The
Svengali grin in the dark, the rough wool suit rustling like bat
wings, the improvised voice describing the empty room full of
windows where Ted died. It sounded like a room where Max
might be headed. And Bruno's mocking impression of some boss
telling Ted—We got a solid rule here son, uh, let me tell you—
sounded as much like an anticipation of Max's fate as a recollection of the dead country singer's.

"Do you know where Ted worked, Martin? At the dog pound.
Someone with his talent working at the dog pound. But they
respected him there. At his funeral all his buddies from work tried
to take him out of the casket so they could waltz with him one last
time."

"Jesus."

"What's Jesus, Martin?"

"I buried that guy."

"You buried Ted?"

"Yah. I'd forgotten his name. But I ripped a good suit throwing his morbid buddies out of my place."

"You buried Ted?"

"He made a pretty memorable corpse. He was extra long, as well as extra gray from whatever he took to kill himself."

"You buried Ted. That's almost a priestly act. You're a priest of the barroom, Martin. Do you realize that?"

Martin realized most readily that he was drunk.

The next thing he realized was that he had missed the edge of the driveway and was breaking a trail through the thistles and what remained of the nuns' depression-era rose bushes. But he preferred mud on his shoes and burrs up the back of his legs to an appointment to the high priesthood in barroom heaven. Under the streetlamp he checked his watch and saw that he still had time to get to the Café des Westens before last call.

Streets

Seventeenth Avenue offered no surprises. The storefronts were full of brass beds and framed prints and software catalogues and hair care products and on and on, all bathed in fluorescent white, flashing hesitant winks his way but not tempting him. Martin passed the old high school where friends of his had gone. A willow tree and a war memorial stood in the center of the big green yard, lilac bushes framed the granite archway over the front doors, a couple of puny irises struggled in the dust. Martin crossed the grass to take a closer look at the monument he'd grown up beside but never read. It wasn't making time for millions as some monuments did, taking in everything from the Boer War to Korea. This piece of granite stopped at commemorating those boys of Western Canada College who, at the dawn of their manhood, died for their country. Martin's eye hopscotched down the list of names. Eaton. Fitzherbert. Gaetz (a European gone back to die on the killing grounds his parents had left). Golding. Hall. Johnson. Musgrove. Pratt. Webster.

There was an older monument hidden behind the big obelisk,

nothing more than a granite box with lichen covering it. It had been tipped and frozen, split open by hard winters.

Up the street he passed an old two-story building with three ziggurat towers where the original owner placed for prosperity the proud emblem of his trade: a milk bottle capped with the slogan MODEL MILK.

Martin crossed over to Eighteenth Avenue and walked by the original Jewish Community Center. Stained stucco and broken windows. Three wooden flagpoles with nothing flying from them. And big black ravens coming out of the eaves in a storm of wings. When they were kids, he and Ostrovsky had played hooky from Sunday Hebrew class by hiding behind the honeysuckle bushes that clung to the cement below the building's stained glass windows. They hid an old coffee tin there, under a pile of broken branches, and snuck through the brush with their pockets full of trash—wrappers, empty cigarette cartons, bits of newspaper—which they stuffed in the tin and lit with long wooden matches. They expected, almost hoped, the smell of smoke and its plume above the honeysuckle would attract the attention of their teachers, but it never did. Each Sunday they narrowly averted a fire in the dry undergrowth and snuck home stinking of soot and soil.

The community center was not far from the old cemetery where Martin's father was buried, watched over now by the row of three-room tar-paper houses across the road. Three rooms with the best view in town of every Jewish burial, of the cars, the crowds, the boxes going down on their ropes and pulleys. A nearly silent descent. At Martin's father's funeral, the rabbi gave a eulogy copied from some book of standard sermons—with all the traditional assurances that a life well lived made way for a place in the afterworld. The rabbi had not known his father and had made no effort to talk to people about him. As the interminable speech wore on, Martin realized that the man would not mention his father's hometown, his adolescent years and marriage in a faraway Polish place. It was as if the rabbi felt that mentioning these things would be an affront to a man who'd died old and comfortable among New World pleasures. Martin remembered tuning the service out so he could concentrate, over the open grave, on his mother's kitchen table stories. The chanting crowd disappeared as he looked hard for a seam, a flaw in the ocean-gray sky and recounted to himself what he knew of the place where his mother had lived, with all the cousins, aunts and half-sisters he could never name. The dark faces on postcard photographs, the diffident mind behind the spidery feet of anonymous handwriting. These old cards were the hiding places of saints. They provided incantations for contacting unburied souls that floated, waiting to be named and recognized.

Their birthplace slept in their children's imagination. Less often, in their children's children's. Buried beneath other dream cities were squares. Spires. Commerce. Hope gone rotten. The proposition of memory was an evil bargain: everything could be kept forever, but it all became corrupt. No pleasure in the having. Martin's mother never really left her Polish town. Walk as she might up and down Calgary streets, their character always described in the negative—they are not as the streets were, the Sabbaths are not so fine . . . the children, the marriages, the taste of ice cream, salami. . . .

Her dreams were more real than her daily business. In them her father stood up from the table, his belly full of dinner. Her sister baked bread. Her children went off to school. Nothing was ever distorted in her dreams. They were not filtered through strange desire or obsession, made grotesque like other people's nightmares. They were very reliable pictures. Almost journalistic. It was the doings of the living that looked strange, and the plain Calgary streets, settled to all others under calm and dust, that appeared distorted. The streetlights reflecting in a green white haze off the buildings. Footsteps sounding magnificently solid, sunken, complete, like the soft forgiving of gravel when a shovel point is thrust in. Lights on in second story windows paling in the moonlight.

The houses all taking on a greenish stain from the streetlamps, some garlanded with unseasonable bulbs that blinked.

Martin wondered what became of his mother's stories when he left her.

They became silent. Presences in a room that could not speak until an audience was found for them. The sun set unwatched, dust settled on tabletops—just dusted—pathways in the carpet were tread a little deeper, the windows went blank and the stories settled with the cobwebs on the ceiling. They roosted for the night, made themselves comfortable in the growing silence till they were fat with it. Ripe and over-opened like blooms in August, they fell and littered the floor.

Except one story, Martin thought, that one I take away with me. I take it with me at the end of each evening. It is my promise to return because it must be put back with the others. It must be back on the following afternoon to rise again through the silence.

He felt incredibly wealthy as he carried it off. This was short-lived and surreptitious wealth, but wealth all the same. Like any other discovery—of uncountable treasure, unmappable lands—his prize was incomprehensible. It made him foolish, full of obsequious worship for a thing he coveted but did not really know what to do with. Martin was like the proverbial lottery winner whose good fortune brings him nothing but elation and an opportunity to squander in style. At best, the story kept him delighted. Captivated. But he could not assimilate it or learn anything by it. He simply had an extra piece of baggage to carry.

Baggage full of clouds.

The leaden clouds that settled over Mlava on a summer day in 1935. One of the very few summer days left to Martin and his mother in their Polish city. Passports had arrived, and there was an ominous date he could not make himself remember on which he and his mother would travel to Warsaw to begin the trip to Canada.

Martin learned the details of their trip long after the fact at his mother's kitchen table. He had no memories of his boyhood in Poland to bring to the aid of the tale. It was as if the boy at the center of it was someone else, not himself. This facsimile of himself even had a different name—Nachman—the name he was first given. But this made the story all the more startling. Hearing it was like suddenly noticing himself in a mirror and not, for the shortest moment, recognizing the image.

So, the clouds. They chased all the market people indoors, caused the stalls to be dismantled and thrown back onto the carts they had arrived on. There was no rain yet, and a thin ribbon of violet stretched along the southern horizon, a sign that there might not be any rain at all. There was another reason, besides the weather, for the ease with which the market goers gave up before the threatening sky. There was a general distraction, a disinterest in business among the Jewish stall keepers who gathered to gossip, held their cashbooks and watched anxiously when a customer moved toward a table. There was a reprieve from the everyday, from the routine of business in the sharing of gossip. And there had been a great deal of gossip in recent weeks about a man named Isaac Rosen, who was dispensing some kind of prophecy from a makeshift stage at the edge of town. His performances were being treated with the same kind of fever and seriousness generally saved for itinerant preachers who presented themselves as the authentic claimant—after so many pretenders—to Messiah-dom. Not that Isaac Rosen made any such claims. But the Mlavers who saw him perform assumed a kind of nervous hush when they described his activities, as if some unwritten law might be transgressed by speaking about them.

As the gossip concerning Isaac grew, stories more mythic than biographic began to circulate about him. He was known to be the son of an old Mlava family, one that had moved to Warsaw when the mill they owned went bankrupt, leaving the family in debt to half the town for supplies they had bought, money they had borrowed, favors they had asked. One particularly angry creditor threatened the elder Rosen at gunpoint, and a mob looted the mill, dragging away planks, rope, doorknobs, axe handles, anything that might be of value, if only as a keepsake to remember the revenge visited on the dishonorable Rosen family.

Isaac was the eldest son of five and the only one who had not been a partner in the unlucky business. He was though, an outcast in his own right, both from his family and from the city. From his family because his father considered him an idler, a schlemiel who used his pitiful scribblings as an excuse not to do real work. Later, Isaac was ostracized by the community because he and the daughter of another prominent Jewish family had carried on a liaison that far exceeded what was conventionally accepted as courtship. The young lovers went for walks that digressed and meandered through parts of the surrounding hills better left to poachers and drawing classes. They were seen dancing, entranced, one gossip insisted, in a tavern in a neighboring town. They were unforgivably bohemian in the face of an utterly bourgeois community. But it was the culmination, not the unfolding of their affair, that left Isaac most scandalized. His lover became pregnant and, without warning him, put herself down on the railroad tracks and waited for the express train from Warsaw to make short work of her shame. Isaac learned of her motives when a letter arrived at his home in which his lover explained herself. The letter was received and opened by his father who suspected incriminating evidence.

The young man was twice devastated, first by the loss of his lover and then again by his inability to understand why she had not relied on him for succor. With the mill on the verge of bankruptcy, Isaac's parents were eager to keep a low profile and urged him to do something, anything, preferably to make plans that included a ticket to a faraway university where he could immerse himself in literary circles, translate Dostoyevsky into Yiddish, smoke opium and do all the things people like him did best. But be far away.

To his parents' dismay, on this one occasion when they encouraged his writing, Isaac had no urge at all to pursue his work. His yearning to write evaporated, buried under the sadness he felt over his loss. A depression overtook him that kept him in bed during the day and turned him into an insomniac at night.

Isaac's father made a final desperate effort to untangle his son from his overused bed, to keep him off the streets where he was harassed by thugs and became the victim of catcalls from neighbors who recognized his mournful lope. Isaac's father knew the man in charge of the network of tollbooths that surrounded Mlava. He had lent the man money, and he proposed the debt be repaid with a favor. There was a tollbooth at the end of Plock Street through which travelers from Szrensk passed on foot and on horseback. The old-timer who manned the booth for decades had died rather carelessly at the beginning of his shift. An innful of travelers slipped into town without paying their toll. One passerby even tossed the remains of his dinner on the man's back, thinking him asleep on the job.

Isaac's father offered him the dead man's job, timidly, almost begging him to take it, fearing that his eccentric son would never take such solitary unstimulating work.

For the first time in weeks, Isaac looked pleased. He told his father he would be glad to take the job. Soon after he began his work as toll collector, his family escaped to Warsaw, barely alive, their personal belongings distributed among their neighbors. And that was the last bit of gossip the townspeople of Mlava shared about Isaac Rosen for almost five years.

Because of Isaac's family history, his reappearance in the rich world of gossip was all the more exciting. But he was spoiled goods, and to return him to the status of a man worthy of the community's eyes and ears, his past was reworked. Mythicized. The impact of what he was doing and saying from his little makeshift stage made a rehabilitation necessary. He hadn't really made the girl pregnant, it was said. She was the type to have lovers on every street. He had nothing to do with his father's business. Thus, he was the only honest Rosen anyone had ever met. And in a final brilliant stroke, certain sources whispered that Isaac was not really his father's son. His birth was declared to be mysterious, inexplicable. No one bothered to ask the beadle, Zanvel Langleben, who registered Jewish births in the town books. Even if evidence of Isaac's legitimacy had been found, it would have been dismissed as a forgery. He was, it was said, the illegitimate son of Hersh of Ostropol, the most illustrious itinerant philosopher of the era, who had traveled from rabbi's court to rabbi's court, leaving for every shtetl he visited a morsel of his wisdom and charity. Isaac, rumor had it, was the offspring of a liaison between Hersh of Ostropol —in his late season—and a much younger daughter of a little known Lithuanian rabbi. This was powerful mythmaking. By setting the impropriety in Lithuania, Mlava's Jews, ever disdainful of their counterparts to the east, could feel free of the taint on the legend.

So now Isaac had a benefactor: the wandering spirit of the Ostropoler Chassid. A somewhat unorthodox benefactor, but one of humility, a walker among the people. One of the Ostropoler's most impressive sayings was making the rounds in Mlava, intoned after Sabbath services and in almost every bar mitzvah blessing:

> The jackal whines when he is hungry,
> every fool has folly enough for despondency,
> and only the wise man can tear the veil
> of being with his laughter.

The sky maintained its gray menace, but no rain fell. The market emptied, leaving the gentile merchants to guess at what was making the Jews so jittery and solemn faced. The road south toward Strezegowo, Racionz, Sierpce, Radzenov and Szrensk was dotted with slow-moving pairs and solitary walkers. There was nothing festive about their pilgrimage. They spoke very little, discreetly checked their watches, feigned curiosity about landmarks in the distance. Everyone wanted to see Isaac Rosen make a spectacle of himself, but no one wanted to appear overly anxious. The rabbi had spoken disparagingly of Isaac's performances, referring to them as the abandoned Rosen's outback theater. No one needed to be reminded that the ritual they were about to take part in under a bare sky smacked of the secular, the unorthodox, possibly of madness.

For the first time in her life, Martin's mother was not engrossed in the concerns and superstitions of the community. She thought instead of the unseen passports that awaited her and her son on some bureaucrat's desk in Warsaw, of the ship that would make the Atlantic crossing, of her husband who was waiting inland in a place called Calgary, Alberta. So distracted was she by these thoughts that she consented to her son's request to carry him on her shoulders. Normally she would have denied him this, saying that when they were with *tata* again he could ride on *tata's* shoulders but not until then. Martin was small, barely five years old, and he spent the ride with a grin on his face, looking off at the swirls of cloud that topped the distant forest.

Isaac Rosen's hesitant parade gathered in a clearing just beyond the last house on the outskirts of town where the landowner had chopped down a cluster of trees to sell as firewood. There was no stage to speak of, and the spectators gathered in a semicircle, filling half the clearing, allowing Isaac as much space to play his drama out in as they themselves needed to watch it.

The sky seemed very low, the mist dropping from it like a veil that came down to cover everything.

Isaac appeared suddenly, dramatically, his hands behind his back, his step quick like a parade-master's, and there could not have been a more incongruous appearance from out of the Radzenover forest. The man stepping out of the birchwood wore a snap-brim hat that covered his eyebrows, a purple suit jacket with thin rounded lapels and tiny white ivory buttons. Standing in his spats and his hat, he looked taller than he was, and gentrified, like a big city poet with a generous patron. No one in Jewish

Mlava had ever gotten himself up in such secular garb. Rosen might have come directly—by hot air balloon perhaps—from some private men's club in Manhattan. Jewish Europe did not seem to have brushed against his suit of clothes. But his black hair, the closely set eyes above a hooked beak betrayed his shtetl forebears. He could spend all he had on the latest styles, but Rosen would never be mistaken for a speculator with Deutsche Marks to burn, nor for a studio boss on an exotic casting call. He was home on the outskirts of the Radzenover forest, dressed like a gangster who had lost his Dusenberg.

The first inclination among the men and women who came to see what Rosen was up to was to sit, shul-style in neat rows. True, this outcast who wanted their attention looked more like a doorman than a spokesman of the people, but they had given up an afternoon's earnings to hear him out, and the customary attention should be paid. But as small groups began to settle themselves down on the grass, the women throwing their skirts around them, the men crossing their legs, Rosen hauled them up one by one and begged them to stand, to mingle, to take a moment's ease because he was not about to offer them a midrash. He had the wings of the Atlantic behind him, he said, the strong wings of the Atlantic, and there could be no sitting now, no sleepy hesitations.

Although Rosen could attract a crowd, he did not enjoy the rapt attention of all comers. A shadow of doubt hung over everything he said. He might have the most stirring report of New World miracles, but his outsiderness lent his whole existence an air of fictionality. He was not understood, and therefore he did not fully exist.

Rosen had a calling card he showed to the men straightforward enough to ask for proof of his connections in America. He handed out copies of a dark photograph of himself and two other men, which was laminated to a piece of heavy cardboard. On the back of the card was a New York City address and phone number under the title ROSEN AND ASSOCIATES: IMMIGRATION EXPERTS—VISAS, PERMITS.

Calling for the crowd's attention, Rosen unfastened his jacket and looked at his pocket watch.

Did he have an engagement in another town? Were they just another audience to him, the folk of his birthplace?

The point of his return was not sentimental, he announced. It was a matter of extreme importance. Rosen admitted it was some-what high-handed and presumptuous to bring everyone away from their day's work like this. He would have preferred to rent a hall in the town, have the *gabbai* set out chairs, print leaflets. But there was not enough time. Certain realities had to be faced with-out the screen of pleasantries.

He stood at first facing the gathering of souls but soon moved into them like a statesman grabbing outstretched hands. And as he left a piece of his pitch with one clutch of men and women, it traveled in mutant form to another group, digressions forming on the original design.

He had come, he said, bringing salvation. A modern salvation—no creaky old creed out of prayer books. He brought word of a New Age, and this age was unfolding in New York City where there were new temples, a new marketplace, a thriving Yiddish press. The city was teeming with life, and the unusual, the unorthodox need not go underground there. He had gone there on a steamer, steerage, with rotten fruit and the trunks of the wealthy—blue tin trunks belted and buckled like little sailors. He would not say how he had afforded the trip or how he had sup-ported himself while he was in New York. Rosen described his stay as if he had been only a spiritual presence in Manhattan—he had not eaten or labored or sweated there, he had not even walked—the underground train took him from doorstep to doorstep. And he had descended, immaculate in his white and black shoes, onto Hester Street. He sailed like a meteor through the observation lounge in the Chrysler Building, raised only a few years before on the corner of 42nd Street and Lexington Avenue. In the ornate roof of this monument he'd discovered a new shrine, wood-paneled, ancient dimples in the carpet where furniture stood, elaborate wire bins where men checked their hats. He shuttled by the sixth-story windows of the old-law tenements on Henry Street where dozens of families were crammed into brownstones. He'd gone down to the Village and listened to sax men play their instruments full of animal scowl. He had watched the morning glory drop its blooms off the EL trestle as the train rattled overhead.

And he had been converted to a new faith. As he spoke these words, hands rose up to cover whispering mouths. Faces in the crowd grew quizzical. It was not easily communicated, the breadth of his faith, the height of it, the fat metaphors that supported it. But Rosen believed that skyscrapers held some transcendent value, that the prospect of thousands of people living and working, tumbled into shining towers, promised a new human possibility. Barbarism was unthinkable, pogroms were unplannable, the hard time-worn life of the ghetto impossible.

In such a place all culture was disclosed to the Jew. Every work imaginable was translated into Yiddish: Wilde, Jules Verne, Heine, Longfellow. Every discipline was available. The end of parochial backwater ignorance! A reinvigoration of the diaspora fire that had been smothered.

The crowd circled aimlessly. Groups of men stood aside to whisper under their breath. Couples slipped away through the trees to begin the walk back to town. Others, like Martin's mother, picked up what they could of Isaac's ravings and smiled politely as he lectured them. Men clasped his hand, patted, as if he were a child with sad pretensions.

Rosen recognized Martin's mother and came toward her with his hands held out. When he was last in Mlava, her husband had already left for Canada, a figure of fun and gossip, and secretly, as well, of admiration.

Taking her hands, Rosen asked Martin's mother if she knew Peretz's story "In the Mail Wagon." She did. It was a plea for women's emancipation, for their right to learn and have an imaginative life of their own. In Canada Peretz's vision has come true, he said. There were not two distinct worlds in the Jewish home— one male, one female. In Canada these two worlds were united. In Canada she would have work and learning. And dignity.

Rosen yanked at his lapels and offered a pantomime of a man bursting with pride. He smiled, then turned away.

As far as young Rivka Binder was concerned, Rosen, the outcast, was not even a good maker of theater. His prosecutor's pose, his earnest eye and the dream he had for her were lost on a calm heart with no desire for new visions. And his faith in a New Age born of office towers, tenement streets, observation rooms with views into the harbor was nothing more than some sweet secular debauchery. It was an urbane *Yiddishkeit* dressed up in gangster clothes that spread the seed of assimilation by way of anecdotes and jazz. The poor man's mind was *eyngelegt,* pickled like an egg.

Very few Mlavers would take a copy of the book that Rosen carried in numbers, Moses King's *Handbook of New York City.* The few copies he had of New York Yiddish dailies were more popular. One or two young men secretly snatched a copy of a booklet that outlined visa and work permit preparations for immigrants. Admitting the desire to go to America or Canada was a bit like an admission of apostasy. To shave beards, teach the children German, hang paintings in the home was something. But to leave home and family?

Rosen's oddball prophecy went down about as well as a snowstorm in June. This kind of concoction was not going to convince the people of Mlava to flee Europe. Everyone knew someone who had left. They had heard stories about life in New York, Chicago, Montreal. Rosen's utopia made them laugh. At least the loudmouthed Zionist who had come through town a month before— calling for carpenters in Palestine—made a bit of sense. But they had a place here by the Radzenover woods.

The afternoon was very still. Isaac looked tired, his shoulder against a birch, hat in hand. He'd used all his best lines. Martin and his mother stood in place where he had congratulated them for their plans to leave. Their neighbors rose and circled them, nodding solemnly as they passed or averting their eyes. Martin's mother took her son by the hand and led him out of the clearing onto the roadway. On the way home people were more animated than they had been when they came. Men gathered in groups and discussed what they had seen. Some scoffed and laughed, their voices carrying over the rippling wheat. Others talked quietly of the scandal, the outrage, the foolishness they had just witnessed. Young Rosen, it seemed, had gone too far, pushed his urgent message a little too hard, and the natural drama of it flipped over into the comic.

"He'll be sorry he quit his job with the tollbooth," more than one walker was heard to say. "There's a future in this?"

Martin's mother kept to the side of the road and made no effort to include herself in any of these discussions. It was at times like this that being without her husband made her feel particularly vulnerable and isolated. And she felt that by including her in his spectacle, Isaac had only called attention to her estrangement from the community. He had made an example of her, and whatever his intentions had been—to lionize, to celebrate, to bully her—none of these had resulted. She felt only that she had been marked as a pariah.

She walked back down Plock Street to the market square and toward her parents' home. Customers who visited her parents' store waved and smiled. Neighbors said hello to her and passed on. Dusk was falling, and the clouds hovered now in the twilight, giant ships full of rain.

This was the night's treasure. A midnight song to keep busy with. Martin repeated it, rewrote it as he marched down Seventeenth Avenue toward last call. He draped it over the storefronts, and put it down on the ground as a rug to walk on. The city

shook and fell before him, disappeared behind the size and wonder of his story. He didn't feel so special. Jericho fell after a horn's
call. Some city somewhere must have fallen for a song.

At the Café des Westens

Something new was going on at the Café des Westens. Martin saw it through the window and stood with his mouth partway open, his face wearing the grim surprised look of a worshiper who finds his shrine desecrated. For the first time in more than thirty years, he considered not going inside. At the back of the room where the old phone booth had been, he could see a band set up on a stage. Ostrovsky went by the window carrying a tray of drinks. Martin gave the pane a smack. His friend passed without hearing, his belly waving.

Martin went inside expecting more disappointments. As far as he could tell, nothing else had changed. The same pockmarked tables and mismatched chairs were scattered around the room. The dusty light fixtures—imitation heraldic shields with bulbs behind them—were still in place. So was the bar with its veneer front and the little toy barkeep keeping watch by the cash register.

But there was a band playing. A drummer batting away at his snare drum, a trombone player sliding his instrument into the ear of the spectator seated nearest to him, a guitarist snapping out arhythmic chords. This was post-Parker jazz. More semibohemia to please the kids who came slumming.

Martin sat on a stool by the cash register and waited for Ostrovsky to come back to the bar. His friend came out of the crowd with an empty tray in one hand, waving with the other.

"Busy night, eh Martin?"

Martin said nothing.

"Something wrong?"

"What'd you do with the phone booth, Ostrovsky?" They had to yell over the music and the whoops and yells of the customers who were dancing.

"I sold it to an antique dealer for eight hundred bucks."

"What do you mean you sold it?"

"I sold it."

"How am I going to call my mother?"

"Call her at home, Martin. I was getting tired of these punks trying to make long distance calls to Istanbul."

"Somebody here knows someone in Istanbul?"

"Nah. They just want to see if anyone will answer." Ostrovsky put a bottle of Scotch and a glass in front of Martin. "See if this lightens you up. You look bleak."

Martin sat glumly and listened as the band finished off a long swing number. He decided they weren't playing it with enough swing era integrity. The rest of the crowd felt differently, dancing and hollering throughout the long piece. One couple did a very good jitterbug.

The fat bus driver by the pickled eggs was humming and snapping and tapping his toes. Some of Max's friends were out in front of the stage dancing. The woman who favored the broken felt hat danced with a long thin character who held a cigarette. He shook ash and smoke through the air as he hopped and twisted. Across the room were three or four familiar faces. Max and Sara weren't among them, but Martin was sure they'd be in to join their friends soon enough. There were a few things he wanted to tell them.

Questions he wanted to ask. The specter of Bruno and his badly preserved monastery hung over him like a bad dream.

Ostrovsky made his way through the crowd to the stage and motioned to the guitarist, who knelt over the edge to talk to him. They nodded at each other and pointed into the dark while the rest of the musicians stood and waited. The stage behind them was a primitivist nightmare—long brass gongs hung from a rack at the back of the stage. Beside them stood a kettle drum looking like a baptismal font and a pair of dusty archaic tuba horns, the intricate hosework in their bellies rusted and green with age. Two matching music stands with little lights clipped to them stood at either end of the stage, and one bare white spotlight crossed it, so the space looked like a tunnel. Behind all this shimmered a gauzy curtain, the color of nightwear in unimaginative porno shows, the goldy pink of fake flesh.

The band regrouped. They were joined on stage by a woman who carried a fiddle, and the trombone player exchanged his instrument for a clarinet. The guitarist stepped off one side of the stage, leaned his guitar against a wall and returned with a chair in one hand, an accordion slung over his shoulder. He put the chair in the center of the stage and sat, hanging his chin over the little keyboard and poking at the keys with his thumb. There was a lengthy tune-up period during which Ostrovsky came over and sat beside Martin. He was beaming, nodding, pointing at the proceedings with raised eyebrows, trying to get Martin's approval. Martin sipped at his drink and smoked, wondering if he should sit with his son's friends and treat them to the same lecture he wanted to give to Max. Something along the lines of: honor thy parents, you unforgiving louts, there's more to life than dance halls and beer. Ostrovsky gave him a poke and pointed at the stage.

The clarinet player was poised at the mike. With one eye trained on the accordion player, he waited for a cue, then with a mutual nod the band broke into a wild eastern European reel that could have been a gypsy folk song. Possibly a Ukrainian harvest dance.

Martin knew the song, and he felt foolish for having dismissed the band so quickly. The musicians were Max's age. The drummer looked younger than Max. But they could really play *klezmer* music. They played the same songs his father had sung along with in their sun room, music that had to be special-ordered from publishing houses in New York and came scratched, on fat 78s in cardboard wrappers. Martin couldn't get over the strangeness of watching twenty-year-olds playing their grandparents' music. He could almost believe it played through them, inexplicably, as if they were nothing more than the tools of song. And whoever dreamed up the arrangements, charted the notes for their willing young lips and fingers, did a magnificent job. The music rose over the crowd like a canopy, drew each woman and man into an intimacy they had not shared when they entered the café, and Martin was swept up in it like the rest.

He edged closer to the dance floor with each song, slowly becoming part of the entertainment. A spectacle himself. He sang and hummed, whispered refrains into his clasped hands. He caught the attention of the musicians, as if they too had come to watch a show, and he was it. The accordion player watched him with one eye. The clarinetist listened to Martin's voice, judged his performance the way the audience judged the band. The woman who played the fiddle bent over and whispered something in the accordion player's ear. He sat on his chair, his music box on his lap, his boots keeping time on the stage. He nodded above the big spread of his machine and smiled, his feet rumbling on like thunder.

When the song ended, the fiddler walked up to the mike that stood in the center of the stage. She pointed across the room at Martin, squinting into the little spotlights that lit up her face. "There's a gentleman here tonight who needs a band, and we happen to be a band without a singer. If he'd agree to it, we'd like to have him up here to join us."

The crowd looked toward Martin and applauded. One hundred

noses turned to see the singer who warranted this invitation. Max's friends stood and cheered, calling Martin's name and urging him to take the stage. Martin was drunk enough to consider the offer. The music made his heart race, and though he knew his voice was only fit to be buried under the roar of a band and the rustle of a room full of drinkers and dancers, he thought that just this once he might find within him his father's tenor, that Ostrovsky's Scotch might loosen it out of his chest. As he weighed the prospect, two of Max's friends came over and took him by the arms. They frog-marched him as far as the center of the dance floor where Martin's misgivings got the better of him, and he started to struggle. He wriggled and elbowed them, twisted until he slipped out of their grasp and made a dash for the side of the room where the tables and chairs were most tightly packed. Laughter and applause followed his escape, as if this were really the performance expected of him, and Martin flopped into a chair —an anchor to keep him fixed in place. The band lost interest in enlisting him and began another song.

Martin sat flushed and huffing, his elbows hooked under the arms of the chair. He was no more than five feet from the table where Max's friends sat. The two who had tried to waylay him were up at the bar getting drinks, and the two women were sitting with their backs to him, heads turned toward each other, talking. Martin heard nothing while the band played. He watched their heads move as words passed, watched the corners of their mouths turn up and down. The woman with the black felt hat did most of the listening. She held a cigarette with the lighted end pointed at the ceiling. A strange sweet smell emanated from it as it burned, but it seemed to maintain its full length for an interminable amount of time.

The band stopped for a break, and Martin settled down to do some eavesdropping. He slumped in his chair and tried to look as inconspicuous as he could. The woman with the hat held her immense cigarette like a torch. Her friend was drunk, excited and she spoke quickly, words piling up on one another.

"It's my favorite building in town. Just off Seventeenth Avenue at Twelfth. I've been waiting for an apartment to open up in it for months. It's a five-story red-brick that's at least seventy years old. There's an art gallery in the basement that's never open, and the front entranceway is the kind you find in Harlem walk-ups where two wings look at each other over the front door and form a voyeur's paradise. I rode the elevator the other night. It's like something in a French film, somewhere you'd get kissed by someone you barely know. With pounded copper side panels and two cage doors—one you open and another that opens on its own. When the car is a floor above you, its wires hang in a big loose tangle from its underside."

Martin wondered how long this could go on. It was the first rhapsody for an elevator he had ever heard. He leaned toward them to interrupt, but there were many more things to celebrate. The woman described how at sunset the windows reflected a patchwork of copper flame, and the brick turned a brilliant red —the color of mesopotamian mud, she said. It looked, as the sky darkened and the sunlight swept along the ground, as if the building were burning from the inside out.

"There's an old yellowed list of instructions explaining how to press the elevator button. The hydraulics sniff and puff as the car comes down. And when you ride, the floors pass you, one after another. They roll by like big granite and rosewood waves. I looked around for open doors to see what the apartments are like, and I stood out on the fire escape on the fifth floor to look at the view." The woman went on to describe the view from the fifth floor—in all four directions—and the cars that sat outside on the street: a Thunderbird, an old Plymouth, a big green DeSoto. . . .

"You know what Sara would say about that." Martin straightened himself up in his chair when the two faces turned. "She'd tell you that de Soto discovered the Mississippi."

The lister of cars turned halfway around in her chair. "She's full of that stuff, isn't she?" She shared her estimation of Sara as much with her companion as with Martin. "She and I are always arguing. We have a different idea of what's worth remembering."

"If it comes down to a decision between American cars and French adventurers, who cares? I hate any kind of trivia." Martin was about to launch into his lecture on the trouble with young people today. He pulled his chair closer to the table, and the two women made room for him between them.

"Oh, come on, Mr. Binder. You must have at least one peculiar interest that nobody else understands."

The woman in the hat put out her cigarette with no end. She watched him with eyes that looked a little bored, but still waited for the answer to her friend's question. Martin looked up at the stage and felt overwhelmed by it again. Bare, blocking the way to the washroom, it had usurped his phone booth. It seemed to be put there as a personal insult to him. He could think of nothing to say.

"My name is Lisa, by the way."

Martin shook her outstretched hand. "I think we've met."

"There must be things you hear of that you just like to remember. We all have things like that."

"I'm not sure I know what you mean."

"I could give you an example."

Martin nodded.

"Well . . . I like it in *On the Road* when a little kid says to his mother, Mama, I'll be a hobo someday."

"What do you like about that?"

"I don't know. It's naive. And honest. Something like killing yourself. It may be the wrong thing to do, but it's still what you really want."

Martin was surprised by the rush of trivia that did come to mind. Anecdotes he collected without knowing it. His memory bristled with little signposts. Louis Armstrong pointing at the guest of honor at a Royal Command performance, saying, *This one's for you, Rex.* Mingus smashing his horn player's hand with a chair because of a bad riff. Marlene Dietrich meeting Orson Welles and telling him, Honey, you're a mess. The time Max admitted that the only word he could remember after three years of French classes was *salut.*

The woman wearing the hat took it off. Her hair was gold and yellow and brown. "You must know so much about Calgary, Mr. Binder. Being an old-timer here."

"I wouldn't say an old-timer."

"When did you come to Calgary?"

"In the thirties, with my family. It was quite a dusty joint back then."

"Not much to do for fun."

"We'd ride the streetcars or hang around the back alleys. If it rained we'd pretend we were fishing in the puddles."

"And you were here during the good years in the sixties."

"That's when I got my business off the ground."

"The funeral home."

"Mm hm."

"A lot of well-off folks must have needed burying back then, eh, Mr. Binder?" Lisa smiled.

Martin took his cigarettes out of his shirt pocket and tapped two onto the table. "You can call me by my first name, Lisa, if you don't mind getting close to an undertaker." Martin lit his cigarette, making a great deal of noise striking the match on the box. Lisa apologized, saying she hadn't meant anything by the remark. Martin offered her the cigarette that lay on the table. He admitted that death jokes came as naturally to most people as breath.

The two men the women had been with earlier shuffled up and sat down. The long thin one congratulated Martin on his singing.

Martin refused the compliment. "I didn't sing."

"We could hear you at the bar from here. None of us knows Yiddish, but we really like the songs."

"My dad used to sing those songs around the house."

The band members were climbing back on the stage. Lisa left Martin's cigarette on the table and took a little paper packet out of her coat. The flame on her lighter was set very high, and it lit up her face, her thick black hair, the buckskin coat she wore pushed back on her shoulders.

She introduced her three friends. The woman's name was Ruth, and the other two were Philip and John.

Martin shook everyone's hand.

There was an uneasy silence. All five looked at one another, smiling and shifting in their chairs. A circle of cigarettes jettied up and down in the dim light, smoke spiraling, but when they had all stubbed out the last bit of a butt, Lisa's still glowed. It gave off a sweet smell that made Martin think of syrup dripped on flame.

The cigarettes came from Cuba, she explained, brought back as part of a romantic overture. She intended at first not to smoke them, to keep them as a memento on the windowsill she reserved for such oddities. But she decided against placing too much importance on a gift whose giver she didn't care for. People would see them on display and ask her when she had been to Cuba, and she would have to admit the source of the gift. Gossip was bound to follow. So she was smoking them as quickly as she could— offering them to everyone who asked—but the silly things were made so strangely, packed so full of tar and resin, that they seemed to burn for hours. It was going to take a long time to get through the whole pack.

She held up the little red and gray package with the name, POPULARES, in elegant script below Spanish words that no one understood.

With the cigarettes she had been given a package of Cuban matches, which were little shellacked twigs topped by a big dollop of something brown that burned. Lisa struck one against the box. It flared, sputtered, and the burning head tumbled off onto the floor. Long Phil put his heel on it.

Lisa admired the sloppiness of the cigarettes with their sweet aftertaste, dropping ash and burnt paper in a little storm around the hand that held them. The box was like a flag. The stink of them like a secret code. The unreadable labels—untranslatable slogans—suggested an affiliation with strange causes. A little revolutionary rune decorated the cover of the matchbox. In red, running crosswise like the spokes of a wheel, a gun overlapped a monkey wrench that crossed the machete used for harvesting cane, and beneath this symbol were the words CIUDAD DE LA HABANA. LISTA PARA LA DEFENSA.

Lisa had another Cuban gift with her: an envelope full of cigar bands. It was decreed in Russian, Spanish, French and German on the flap of the envelope that everyone should collect Havana cigar rings.

The bands went round the table like a stack of family photographs. They were brown and red with gold embossed details, the little portraits in their centers surrounded by more untranslatable slogans. HOYO DE MONTERREY. POR LARRANAGA. LARA IMMENSA. One brand portrayed Simon Bolivar, his brocaded collar up high around his chin, HABANA, strung like a necklace, in block letters on his chest.

Habana was a rare recognizable word. And there were a few brands with decipherable names. Capulets and Romeo y Julieta. Long Phil, with a memory that trapped detail the way a crypt held on to a corpse—he remembered what color socks a friend wore the day they met—thought that a character in a Mordecai Richler novel smoked these. Namesake of star-struck lovers, the Romeo y Julieta came out late in the evening with a Scotch, a symbol of ennui and urbanity.

John and Long Phil chose a favorite from the set, singling out the largest red and gold band. The label advertised a brand called Fancy Tales of Smoke. John fondled the little label until Lisa said he could have it. He and Phil began to guess at what the name might mean to a smoker familiar with the brand. What stories it commemorated.

"Fancy Tales of Smoke," they shouted, improvising variations and inventing scenarios for a book full of daydreams.

They pushed their chairs back and became part of the general club din as they argued about an appropriate heroine and hero, the locale and the weather that would suit their fancy tales. Phil produced a pen, and these variations were set down on a pile of unfolded napkins.

The clarinet player practiced long wistful riffs on his instrument. The rest of the band seemed to be waiting for him to quit. They leaned on mike stands and fooled with the scraps of paper on their music stands.

Martin looked at the young people he was sitting with and wondered what Max told them about him. That he was a drunk? That he had no interests other than his family? They seemed to regard him as some kind of relic, a sepulcher full of secrets about the past. Anything could be discussed before him, any boring piece of trivia worked over. He was like the sphinx with stone ears. He did feel rather old and rough, sitting in his sportshirt, drinking his Scotch, surrounded by all the young couples who laughed, sipped mauve drinks and waited to dance. In the old days, before Max was born, Martin and his friends had gone to dinner clubs and waltzed around on the parquet floors, the fake crystal chandeliers dripping little diamonds down the walls.

Lisa watched Martin over her cigarette. She looked uncomfortable, as if she regretted bantering with her friend's father. "Tell us more about your work, Martin."

"My business?"

"Yeah, what it's like."

"What can I tell you? It's a good business."

Lisa took a nervous drag.

"It's just up the road. I'll take you to see it if you're interested."

The drummer gave a little celebratory drum roll. It looked like the band was about to start. Apart from Lisa, Martin's companions acted as if they hadn't heard his offer. Long thin Phil asked if anyone wanted another drink. John mimicked the drummer with two fingers on the tabletop.

"Sure. It might interest you. I did it all for Max and his mother."

Lisa nodded emphatically. She was trying very hard to make up for her badly received death joke. "I'd like to see it."

Long Phil shot her a look of horror. His friend looked at his watch. "It's late, Lisa. A little too late to visit a funeral home, don't you think?"

"Nah." Martin stood up. "It's very campy. You'll love it."

The band worked away at something they called "Yiddish Blues." Martin gathered up the napkins with their doodlings, folding them into a little packet, as if he were helping Ostrovsky by tidying up the mess they'd made.

The Republic of Letters

The night had a flaw in it. There was, in the mid-August air, the taste of autumn. The trees were unconvincing in their leafy wealth. And the snapdragons and marigolds—glowing purple and yellow beneath streetlamps—all had rotten brown undersides. Surely a carefully attuned ear could hear them bending and screaming in the cool air. The pique of summer was off. What remained was a front. Couples in shorts dressed as they did out of habit. They let the cool breeze travel up their thighs, imagining soft night hands. Heaters whirred in topless cars. The night was irretrievably distant from the day, the cool blackness wore such a different dress from the city's bright yellow suit at noon. Silver clouds rolled back on the edges of the city.

What will the city bring? everyone was asking. *And what must I bring to it?* Men and women said this again and again into their upturned collars and mumbled it into clenched fists. They blew these questions up at the sky in the smoke from a cigarette and rolled them down the driveway with the garbage. Something was required as an offering to make the summer stay. But the right gift had to be found, the weight of the sky had to be propped up on upraised hands. And every soul approached this labor in its own manner. With different degrees of urgency, different disciplines.

Max and Sara kissed beside a green DeSoto, unaware of its significance. They kissed with the urgency of young lovers who have not had so many kisses, who have not tired of tongues, who still believe that a kiss must be long to be good, so that there is the possibility of shortness of breath, the slightest promise of suffocation. This was desire practiced as a kind of romantic leap into the unknown. The longer the kiss, the greater the chance that someone might lean out a window in the building that rose from the curb behind them to admire their passion. Such a spectator might even become aroused at the window ledge, with nothing on below the waist, the unacknowledged partner in a ménage à trois.

Possibilities were all around them: windowsills that begged for elbows, porches where chairs creaked, darkened cars where radios played. The city was a theater for their love. A long promenade to be paraded down. And the theater they made together was more traditional than they knew. It included all the proper ornaments and rituals.

Sara wore violet-blue eyeliner, bright red lipstick, the outlines of her mouth made dark, as if etched on by some skill she would not reveal. At least not to Max.

Together they walked along back streets and alleys, drunk and tired, each laughing at everything the other said. The air smelled of cut grass. Possibly the last cut the season would demand.

When they arrived at the Café des Westens, the band was finishing its last set. The dance floor was empty, and the musicians seemed to be playing for themselves, the drummer grinning as he batted his snare, the clarinetist, eyes closed, blowing his solos into some corner of the room known only to himself. Sara and Max took a table by the window and watched as cars drove by. The woman who lived in the house across the street was framed in her picture window with her little book, the bulb over her head throwing a bright halo.

Ostrovsky came up to them and shouted over the music. "What can I get you kids?"

They ordered four draft to make sure of a second round before the café closed. Ostrovsky said nothing about Martin. Neither when he took their order nor when he returned with it. He was determined not to be the one to tell Max his father was drunk this evening. He set the four glasses down on the table, smiled at Sara and asked, *"Ver is di sheine angekante?"*

Max and Sara returned blank stares.

"I said, 'Who is this beautiful stranger?'"

"You know Sara, Ostrovsky."

He clasped the tray under his arm, next to his heart and feigned surprise. "Oh, but she looks so marvelous tonight I didn't recognize her."

Max and Sara sipped at their drinks to hide embarrassed smiles. Ostrovsky ambled off to answer to an anxious customer who was yelling, "Waiter, waiter," as if his life depended on his next drink. The band members began packing up their instruments, rolling sheet music into cardboard tubes and gathering up electric cable.

There was a rap on the window. Max and Sara turned. Two men stood with their faces very close to the glass. One looked away from them and down the road, but his partner held up a sketch pad and pointed at Sara with his pen. There was a permit clipped to the front of the pad with the City of Calgary crest at the top, which listed the streets and hours when the man was allowed to practice his craft. The light falling through the café window onto the street made it easy for Max and Sara to see out, but the drawer squinted, as if he were already sizing up the difficulty of portraying his chosen subjects in the half-light. The man had his long black hair tied in a ponytail. His high cheekbones, his dark complexion, the long oriental slant of his eyes made him look like a furious deity. He held up five fingers.

Max shook his head.

The drawer subtracted his thumb to show four.

Max smiled and shook his head again. The drawer's friend ambled around on the sidewalk behind him, his hands deep in his pockets, his shirttail out.

Three fingers.

Max shook his head. No.

Two.

Max nodded.

Couples seated beside them began to notice what was going on and got up from their seats to watch.

Sara covered her face with her hands. "Max. Do you have to?" Then they sat, part of the time trying to look at ease, part of the time setting themselves at the proper angle to show their best profile. Their reflections appeared jerky in the window, and behind the glass the drawer's eyes, narrowed in concentration, traveled up and down from their heads to his pad.

There was mumbling in the café about price; doubts were aired about the drawer's ability; someone remarked that the man ought to get back to Eighth Avenue before his bench got taken. Max and Sara sat trapped under the artist's stern gaze, saying nothing, baited by the promise of close attention, made forgiving by the man's obvious need but doubtful still that anything would come of his work. Their neighbors leaned with elbows on the edges of tables, got up on tiptoe to see what was being done. One woman announced over and over, "I want one, I want one," as if the repetition of her wish would bring it about.

When the drawer had finished, he flattened his pad against the window. Max and Sara were paired with fat-lined characterless versions of themselves—necks too long, eyes too soft, their features made almost identical—as if the man could not really tell one Caucasian from another. Sketch-Max could have been any boy, nose pressed to a shop window. Sketch-Sara was distinguishable, barely, as a woman by the length of her hair and a slight pucker in the lips. Not even the deep lines that ran from her nose down to her chin were visible.

Max got up to pay what he'd promised for the drawing to a chorus of "Let us see it," "Is it any good?" "I want one too."

The drawer came up very close to him on the sidewalk, narrowing his eyes as he had when he was concentrating on the sketch. Max felt as though he were being sized up and dismissed at the same time. The man said, "Gimme three bucks man, I'm real poor."

Max handed him a two dollar bill and took the drawing. He looked for Sara in the window, but she had disappeared. He looked instead at silver-edged white letters etched on the glass—Café des Westens—which struck him then as his father's most authentic signature. The drawer followed a passerby up the street, trying to scrounge up more trade.

Max unrolled the drawing. In one corner the man had made a heart with two broad crests at its top and a soft little point at the bottom. Inside the heart, words difficult to read because of the fast broad strokes with which they were made appeared to say, "Love comes around too soon before it goes." Max looked up the street and saw the drawer's partner, his pants down around his knees. The man was pissing, carefully aiming the long arc of his water at some special point, as if a certain place had to be marked.

Max realized he had paid for the drawing with his last two dollars, and he wondered if Ostrovsky would let the tab go by. Then he counted up the change in his pockets, and to this he added the value of the postage stamps that were pressed into a little collage of wildlife and moonmen at the bottom of his wallet.

A Tour

Up the road, thinking of his empty-pocket son, Martin marches with his pilgrims. He smokes and marches, the tip of his cigarette drawing bright orange portraits on the breeze. His breeze, for more than fifty years, and his streets, so he paints them any way he likes. Martin never thinks about what the city means to him, about his lifelong attachment to it. He does not puncture his accomplishments and attachments by submitting them to endless scrutiny. He lets his work be. He is quite whole, like an iceberg or a juggernaut that may not be in control of its own travels but plows along all the same. And being this, his son remains for him an enigma, a strangely unformed figure performing a dangerous balancing act. Martin imagines Max as the possessor of eyes that gaze out of a crowd, the one character in a scene who is frozen in self-reflection while all those around him are caught in a carnival of flight and fury. He imagines that to Max the city is an experiment under glass, every bit of which has to be studied closely just to be known. Never, by any stretch of the imagination, to be made his own. That was out of the question. There was too much beyond

Max, too many things he loved but never felt were his to hold. The contradictions he saw in everything kept him one step removed from it all. His son cultivated an ironic distance between the world and himself with as much care as any craftsman applied to a trade. The café was a part of this work, a place to listen to old and nearly extinct music and savor the irony of doing so. Make an ennui-ridden smile.

Martin looks at his pilgrims, the two women close behind, sometimes taking each other's hand. The two hesitant young men dawdle, read the headlines on newspapers through the glass in the corner boxes and miss cross lights on purpose.

Martin considers his pilgrims and what the Café des Westens is to them. The music, meaningless. The players dressed in their mock-shtetl attire, their black suits and spotty white dress shirts taken for the costume of just any rumpled wedding songsters. The squeal of the clarinet mistaken for the sound of just any jazz, mistaken for Bird and Coltrane and a hundred other names heard of but recognized no further. The shtetl whine forgotten, the wistful pleas to something higher in all this minor chord lamentation no longer heard. The accordion player made himself up as a bit too much of a modern musician, his hair cut like a bad hairdresser's version of a Mozart wig, his stance at the microphone a little too removed, too passive. He maintained an aloofness more appropriate to a Berlin nightclub than for singing Yiddish wedding songs.

Martin and his troupe pass a strip joint named Bubbles. A swarm of blue-suited businessmen stand out front whacking each other on the back. They smell of smoke and liquor. Lisa turns Martin around and points.

"If you stop," she says, "you'll see a tree. Behind that tree is the cupola that sits on the roof of the building I was telling Ruth about."

Martin sees at least thirty trees and no cupola.

"I walked around the place," she adds, "and looked into all the windows to see what kind of art the tenants hang on their walls."

"It's a little strange, isn't it, Lisa, to carry on such a close relationship with an apartment building?"

Martin doesn't listen to her answer. He is not really interested in Lisa's personal philosophy, which has something to do with fetish and art and architecture and love. The latter, according to Lisa, in some theoretical sense—so Martin gleans as he watches the traffic—has a great deal to do with all the former items.

There are a lot of walkers out for a late hour in Calgary. Couples whisper to each other as if they are traveling down the aisle of a great cathedral. Men in trucks play their radios loud.

"How about love, then?" Martin can't keep the sarcastic tone out of his voice.

"Love's no different, Martin."

"Oh."

"Love's the same."

He leads his pilgrims—two willing, two skeptical in their devotion—across his parking lot. The sweet smell of disinfectant hovers over the empty lot. The asphalt is pristine, black like the side of a volcano. And he thinks. This, he thinks, is no different from the café. This is my café. The confusion over who is doing what is the same wherever youth and experience keep wary company. The old wonder how the young can be so ignorant and yet so attractive. The young wonder how the old can be so strange and so old. We are always out of one another's reach.

Martin stops the foursome by a door and raises his keys up to a light to find the right one. A police car rolls by, and the driver honks.

"Martin?"

"Hmm?" He looks over his shoulder at Lisa and stands away from the knob where he is forcing a key.

"What are we doing here?" She watches the police car disappear around the corner.

"You said you wanted to see my place."

She closes her eyes and sighs. It would be best to tell him the truth. That she didn't mean this. That the agreement to visit was all she had to offer, since the idea of it might settle things, while the visit itself can only stir things up. She wishes he would realize this for himself.

But Martin's instincts are useless before young hearts, his common sense dull. His presumptions cause a blockage of blood to the brain. And he cannot get past the idea of Lisa. Or the idea of Sara. Or of Ruth. Little idols they are to him, each with their particular attributes and powers. And what they could become! Ruth, leaning against his geranium boxes, the flowers' smell around her like the reek of balm, is a sphinx, the splendor of Memphis, rose in her cheeks, green eyes. She seems to him sated and knowing, aware of her beauty, told so many times of it that she has become it. He sees nothing besides this. Surrounded though he is by the others and the geraniums' night-smell and the one crazy bird up in a poplar tree, squawking, as if it doesn't know what time it is.

Martin is surrounded too by the idea of Sara, which follows him everywhere, fixed and fierce, inescapable like a bird's noise. It is a song that preys on him. The idea of Sara begins as a bare melody and flourishes, opens up, booming and crashing like a terrible symphony. She takes many shapes in his imagination: an idol out of *Gilgamesh,* a handmaiden from "The Song of Songs." She appears as a wisp of light escaping from a lamp, as a puzzled face tiled into a temple floor. Bronze, sienna, sky blue and gold. These fantasies all travel with him as elaborate glosses on Sara's hair, on her almond eyes. They are extrapolations drawn from the mystery of elegant arms. She sends away loneliness. He realizes she is privy to a great deal of information because she is a kind of alchemist.

The dream of her trails behind him into the big garage, where he keeps the Cadillac hearses, and alights on one of the long white rooftops as he ushers Ruth and Lisa and their two companions inside. There is much foot shuffling and jingling of change in pockets. Martin turns on the lights.

"The cars," he says. "Four black, two white. I'd take the black ones any day. They remind me of John F. Kennedy and royalty on parade. The white ones seem to be very fashionable these days, which I can't understand, since the black ones are black. Basic. The white ones disappear beside a snow drift. They vanish in the heat. And since you've already got one vanished goddamn body on board, it's beyond me why you'd want any more bodies to vanish."

Martin's audience lines up, backs against the wall. Captive. He smooths his hair down and motions for them to follow. From the garage they enter a waiting room with a sofa and a wet bar. Martin calls this room the lounge. The light is sleep-inducing, a shade darker than tangerine. Martin waves an outstretched hand from one end of the room to the other, gesturing as if he is selling something, as if the scene is attached to the wrong sound track, and he ought to say, "A beautiful living room/dining room set, Mrs. Brown."

But instead he rambles.

"Nobody appreciates my renovations or the picture with the mayor. The wallpaper is new, and the molding." He runs a thumb along a groove in the woodwork. "When we reopened, the mayor came with his wife, and they both said this was the nicest funeral home they'd ever seen."

Martin's four charges bump into one another and get squashed two to a doorway, Laurel-and-Hardy style. They are too nervous to talk, so they march obediently after Martin in the tangerine light, trying to convince themselves that it is not odd to be taken on a tour of a funeral home by its drunk proprietor at one o'clock in the morning. It is a matter of respect for a friend's father.

Martin leads them to an elevator and suggests they visit the second floor, but Long Phil asserts himself for the first time since the tour began. He will not go upstairs. Death has become too obvious a theme, and their guide for the evening has acquired a sinister air. Gestures that seemed pathetic now appear suspect. Friendliness might really be ill will dressed up to look nice.

Martin's hair sticks up from being mussed with too much, and one side of his shirt collar points at the ceiling. He is drunk enough to become a little panicked and distracted, tired and worried by a sense of vulnerability.

But time moves very slowly, the way it does when a car leaves the road, and the moment during which the hulk sails through the air and flips like a trick plane seems to last for hours. The orange corridors wind around a honeycomb of anterooms and innumerable bathrooms with huge porcelain tubs. Porcelain floors under the tubs. Porcelain walls. The wallpaper becomes more lurid. The carpet grows thicker, an onrushing tide, and there may be the smell of ocean, or at least drowning, on the stale air. There is the constant hum of air conditioners, the rising and dimming of lights as Martin introduces each section of the building.

After what feels like hours of this, Martin offers them a drink and a seat in one of the two-seaters in the orange lounge. But no one feels like sitting or drinking, and they move on, down halls they've already seen.

Martin disappears through a doorway. He is far enough ahead of his group that when he turns the corner his voice breaks off. The lecture he has been giving about the routine of his business, its reliability, especially in hard times, is cut short by the wall he has disappeared behind.

And as they join him, pressed up against the wall, they see the corpse that lies in its elegant mahogany box. Martin talks on like a patient whose tongue has been loosened by therapy. One by one, Lisa, then Ruth, then the two silent young men, go over to look at the spectacle, which is real, very real, but somehow unbelievable —so lifeless, the face garishly painted—as if the body might be a hoax. A trick done with mirrors. The head is very old and gray, and it is a touch larger than it ought to be, a bit bloated. A blue moon waiting to be rolled out for those who knew it in another phase.

Martin talks on as if it isn't there. He talks about Edith and her work habits. How she drives customers away with her smoking and her catalogue of death jokes. "This is some repertoire," Martin says. "This is the repertoire of a woman who has been harangued and spoiled into a little world of her own that has no fixed rules or expectations. She just makes things up as she goes along."

Lisa and Ruth have already scuttled out of the room. John and Long Phil are bent over the casket posing as mourners. They may, like any red-blooded boys who discover a tomb, be looking for treasure.

Martin gives the subject of Edith a rest, reassembles his gang of four and walks them across a little foyer to the back of the funeral home's chapel. He holds his hands behind his back. An unlit cigarette hangs from his mouth.

"What's your favorite hymn?" He looks from face to face. His hands go through his pockets after a match. "Tell me your favorite hymn." Ruth and Lisa are quiet. John and Long Phil laugh nervously, but Martin interrupts them and asks again, a little irritated, "Don't ya know any hymns?"

Lisa, still trying to be helpful, suggests "Rock of Ages." Ruth explains that she and her friends are either Jewish or atheists, or both. Martin opens the louvered door that hides his tape collection and the elaborate stereo system. He presses buttons, and as green and red bars of light blink on the machine's face, he looks through his selection of cassettes for the night's first request. He cues up the song, and "Rock of Ages," played slowly with a backbeat, blares from the speakers.

Martin thinks this is impressive. But he is the only one smiling. The other four look at him a little aghast, with expressions signaling that he should turn the volume down. And in their faces—which are sad, mouths open just a little, eyes narrow with concern—he finds the answer to his wonderings about who he is to them. What he is really.

He is Autumn.

Autumn. With his twill pants one shade darker than his barley colored shoes, his shirt collar peaking in a clean white line into one of the deep furrows in his neck. His hair thinning, so that when it is combed it looks forever wet, running in runnels down the side of his head, over the crown, the blond of youth now dusty, russet-colored, like the bank of fallen leaves around a tree.

To them he is the sad late season. He is gray skies, smokey air and a reminder of all that must be done before the coming cold.

The Room in Sunlight

"The daily meeting place for artists in Berlin was the Café des Westens on the corner of the Kurfurstendamm and Joachimsthaler strasse, nicknamed by those in the know as the Café Megalomania. Ernst Blass described it in the days before the First World War: 'I still remember the café in all-powerful Berlin. The drowsy gaslight. Lots of people with determined faces. Newspapers and waiters. Just as it ought to be. . . . What was in the air? Above all Van Gogh, Nietzsche, Freud too, and Wedekind. In our circle we had been sailing in Expressionistic waters for a long time. It meant the courage of one's own means of expression; the courage to be oneself. . . . But which self, that was the confusing thing.'"

Sara stops reading. She rests her head on her fist. Her hair hangs over her arm and hides it. Her makeup, left from the night before, casts a charcoal shadow around her eyes. She reads from a big book with blue covers.

The book is full of photographs of Weimar-era Germany. Bowler-hatted songstresses in pinafores fronting all-black jazz bands, trombones pointing skyward. Crowds of smiling Nazis making a bonfire of books. An organ grinder with his monkey on his shoulder described as "an unemployed man." The big moon head of Weill, preexile Brecht tipping the cap of an erstwhile Mac the Knife. Hitler and Hindenburg seated on a dais, the old general's moustache drooping in the afternoon heat.

Sara slides the book over to Max so he can see each photo.

She starts to recite again. "The daily meeting place for artists in Berlin was the Café des Westens." Sara is enthralled by her discovery. She wants to know whether Ostrovsky named his restaurant by accident or with intent.

Max doesn't know. He can only guess. He tells her what his father has told him. That Ostrovsky is a plain man. A dynamo with no conscience to speak of. A survivor. He runs on a kind of brute vitality, carries a huge load, is productive in all seasons. A human locomotive with charm. These clichés are the patina lying over the great scaffolding of story that he is made of.

Ostrovsky appeared as a relatively ordinary descendant at the end of a bizarre and unorthodox line of Polish Jews. He was the only son of a butcher whose father was a doctor whose father was a false messiah. A minor false messiah that is, a stirrer of trouble in a few villages, not a full-fledged engineer of chaos and property liquidation. The messiah's son—the doctor—led an obscure group of renegades from respectable medical practice who treated the criminally insane in a converted nobleman's castle near Warsaw. The doctor's son, Ostrovsky's father, was a maverick of a different sort. He earned his living hacking *treyfene fleysh*—nonkosher meat —in a town where no Jew would taste it. Some were forced to eat *treyf* during their term in the Polish Army, but just as many starved themselves on beets and potato gruel.

Ostrovsky's father worked as a cook for a detachment that rode maneuvers and camped in forests. His family scratched his name off the list on the inside cover of the prayer book where births were noted. He had chosen a life even the unorthodox would not tolerate. He learned his trade slaughtering lame horses and stray livestock with a bayonet and sometimes a saber. This heritage had become difficult to celebrate. The manly code that once framed it had fallen into disrepute. Slaughterhouses were no longer part of the commonplace of human travail. Meat reminded people of murder. The scenario of the elder Ostrovsky disemboweling lame horses prompted diatribes from men and women who rested a hand on leather belts, who scuffed nervously with leather soles. So Ostrovsky tried to put a sheen on his soiled patriarchy when he described these things to Martin. Degrees of cruelty, he insisted, were difficult to discern with regard to butchery. A gleaming cleaver and a clean countertop have only the advantage of being more comfortable to work with.

Ostrovsky is the image of his father, short and thick-shouldered, a little pear shaped. An old-timer who knew Ostrovsky's father in the old country remembers how he looked on his outdoor assignments for the Polish detachment of horse. Often laboring by twilight under a newly risen moon, he might have inspired Caravagio, the fleshy arms working metal hard against bone, sweat dripping into a dusty clearing.

Ostrovsky's greatest disappointment is the smallness of his life. He feels diminished by the spectacle of his father's career, as if he were a paler version of the man he resembles.

The elder Ostrovsky went by his Polish name—Pavel—rather than the Yiddish, Feivel Yehuda, he was given at birth. Under this disguise he could blend into the community of men he traveled with and gain their trust.

His confidence would surely have evaporated if one wily companion had called him by his true name. The scholar's name, the namesake of *shochetim*. It was not a name to survive with in the wild.

But there was something in his rough character that inspired respect. Nobody thought to address Pavel by any name other than his adopted one. He became a companion and an advisor to the hetman of the Polish detachment of horse. He was relied upon for weather predictions, for instructions on points of Russian and Turkish geography, for the ingredients of medicinal balms that would ward off hunger and bronchitis. He told magnificent lies, all of which were believed, about concoctions with the power to reattach severed limbs and return eyesight to the blind. If only he could find all the necessary ingredients, he would produce his magical balm for the hetman of the detachment to see. But these things could never be found all at once. He recited the long list of items like a pharisee doing his priestly duties: he would need ribwort, thyme, speedwell, primula, burnet, yarrow, sage, mallow, elder. He remembered from his childhood readings in the Haftarah all the things required for the historic burnt offerings, the guilt offerings, the peace offerings and the jealousy offerings. He set these ingredients into new order as part of his miraculous elixir. Take the anointing oil, he would say to his baffled commander, and put with it the olive oil and frankincense, and then at the appointed time take two turtles or two young pigeons (turtles and pigeons were interchangeable) and use the innards of them. Then add cedar wood and hyssop with scarlet. All this was a cure for plague or leprosy or scall, but more would be required if the mixture was to ward off demons—two oxen, five rams, five he-goats, one young bullock—and he went on to create the most far-fetched mixture, one he knew he would never be called upon to make. The crowning ingredient of this potion was a dollop of balsam oil extracted from the ancient persimmon plant, now thought to be extinct, which grew in the area of the Dead Sea near Qumran.

Pavel Ostrovsky's lies were so extravagant and full of uncheckable facts that his pronouncements went completely unchallenged. He was looked to for an explanation of all things unpredictable. And his reputation grew to the point where he was taken for some kind of holy man, a shaman, though he was really a meat hacker with a big mouth.

It was a bit of good fortune that Pavel found one day, in an abandoned house where he and his companions spent an unusually cold spring night, a few needles and a jar of ink: the remnants of a tattooist's trade. At first he felt nauseated. They looked to him, in the drawer where he found them, like relics in a bogus shrine. Like toenail clippings, bones, pig's knuckles posing as the leftovers of saints.

But he took them, packed the ink and needles with his knife in a leather bag and went about learning how to use them from descriptions offered by men who had been tattooed. And so he attained another craft that elevated him above the rest of the detachment. He now not only took care of the hungry, but decorated them, prettied the wandering soldiers who missed the few precious possessions that in better times satisfied their desire for beautiful things. Their dovecote and bed stand, their water bowl and beer stein, the decorated jackets they left behind for their wives to wear.

The particular *esprit de corps* that flourished among his companions called for a fairly limited array of tattoos. Small crosses were in demand, and a dovish bird to signify the Holy Ghost. Pavel also mastered an assortment of unorthodox symbols that he hoped to deface his companions with. Apes, leopards, tigers, cats, storks, peacocks, panthers and gazelles were some prohibited beasts— symbols of iniquity—that he offered to god-fearing Polish boys.

But it was not his companions in the detachment who were most drawn to this exotic catalogue. Such oddities were wildly popular with the cossack riders who roved in bands on the outskirts of the surrounding towns. Pavel could never distinguish among them—whether they were Ruban or Don or Terek Cossacks. Each man who visited him looked as fabulous as the one before, with a lambskin hat at a terrific jaunty angle upon a head as ruddy and imposing as any he had ever seen. The black and gray beards thick and full as Persian rugs, teeth yellow and crumbling.

These Cossacks heard somewhere of the man who tattooed

Polish conscripts. They might well have killed one young draftee Ostrovsky's father had tattooed and, hanging his body like a trophy on a tree, become transfixed by the surprise on his chest. A fine filigreed cross on his shoulder. An illicit tiger on his thigh.

Overnight, Pavel of the Polish detachment of horse was in demand. Hetmen rode up to where he and his companions camped and demanded to know what he received in exchange for his work. They sat in his tent or on a stump in the sun, arms bared, waiting to be decorated.

Ostrovsky's father admired and hated them. He believed in their heroism. He believed that Don Cossacks cast their capes like a black carpet over the ice near Rostov and rode across with muffled steps to attack their enemy's rear. He believed it was beautiful, despite the outcome, that Cossack cavalry played cat and mouse with tanks. He also knew they robbed banks, ambushed transports, waylaid grain collection detachments. He knew that victims of Cossack raids were flayed alive, split open, clubbed to death, roasted on coals, that infants were buried alive while bottles were raised to the spectacle. And it was no exaggeration, he knew, that the bowels of women were opened by these picturesque men, that live cats were inserted into the wounds before they were sewn up.

Ostrovsky's voice wavers as he remembers how his father described these things. It was as if the son also saw each quick needle prick on the hetmen's arms, saw his father betraying his hatred to each resplendent hetman's back as he set the ink oozing under ruddy skin.

It isn't easy, Max says, to understand Ostrovsky's relationship with the past. He is not nostalgic. He is not burdened with regret. But then again, the past contains him. It talks him and walks him around. Possibly he knows why he gave his restaurant its name. Possibly it named itself.

This clears nothing up. It is the kind of Sunday morning patter Sara has heard before, and she watches Max watch her, becomes aware of herself breathing and returns to her book. It is open at a full-page photograph of a very sad-eyed bohemian who looks tall in his long jacket and baggy trousers. He wears enough material to cover a circus tent. He is slim, his collarless shirt tucked under his belt, and he holds a leather satchel in one slender hand. The other hand is deep in a pocket. His shirt-sleeves do not show under his coat sleeve. His brow is lowered before the camera, his full lips pursed as if he would rather not be seen. He is a beauty. Somehow a kinsman of Sara's, and Max watches her move a finger over the bohemian's arms down to the bag he holds. She is still, except for the finger that travels along one lapel and over a daguerreotype cheek. She brushes his sepia hair.

Max watches her eyes. They narrow, and the long lines that run from her nose to her chin make her look ancient, carved.

He turns from where she caresses the boy with his lonely lapels toward the wall and the window blind. The sunlight finds its way through the cracks in the burlap. Max counts the little glimmering bodies in Sara's pinprick galaxy.

He takes the phone up off the floor and puts it beside him on the bed.

"Who are you calling?" she asks without looking up from the book. The pages turn. Goodbye to the young beauty and his empty leather bag. Now welcome Heinrich and Thomas Mann, both in overcoats and hats. Heinrich wears a goatee and a bow tie. His brother, a dark moustache and spats.

"My grandmother." The line rings and rings, so Max hangs up and dials again. He lets it ring fifteen times. He thinks of the phone sitting in his grandmother's den, on the old record player in its walnut box. The record slots full of Cantorial selections and *La Traviatta* on old 78s. The phone ringing underneath the orange and yellow dahlias and asters his grandmother clipped and put in the Chinese vase Max gave her on her eighty-first birthday. She might be out for a walk or clipping more asters in the back-yard, shooing the cat with its mangy orange eyebrows.

And she might not hear the phone because her ears are tuned to street noise no one else can hear, the hawkers shouting about their late afternoon leftovers, the *drozhkis* rattling by in a cloud of dust, the top-hatted men with their severe wives on their arms, young men in Polish Army uniform stepping as firmly as they can on the wooden sidewalk so that their new boot heels ring across the square.

All this went on outside the door of her father's house. The big black form in the front window was her father, Reb Menachem, his coat on, his wide-brimmed hat in his hand, the window cringing just a bit for being looked through by him.

Reb Menachem, considering prairie, cattle and rimrock.

Because it is Friday afternoon, before the Sabbath, and the air is already full of the smell of *cholent*, of potatoes boiling, frying onion, the thick rising steam of meat rolling in a pot, Reb Menachem Mendel is hesitant about making the trip to his leasehold. He is hesitant most of his days, the kind of man who will get into a cupboard when thunder is shaking the eaves, who retreats to his library when the children are making too much noise, who conveys his learning—which is as wide, it is said, as the gray ocean between Odessa and Sevastopol—in a modest halting manner, turning the pages of Talmud slowly, allowing no obvious flourish to enter his subtle movement between bits of text, leaping as a squirrel does from one limb to another, to offer an interpretation so clear and so full it seems to have preexisted the text it is meant to discuss.

Reb Menachem is by no means an overwhelming presence in his home. At times it is not hard to forget he lives in the house at all. Half the day he is surrounded by children at his *cheder* table. Behind the counter of his family's dry goods store he is so self-effacing, stern and reliable that he seems less like an animated presence than another archaic tool of measurement. A tall bearded scale. A scoop with more than one handle. The jinn of the counter. He maintains a great gray silence as he doles out handfuls of treats

—dates, figs, carob, peanuts and pistachios—as he takes down jars of sweets and counts out six purple, six black, the rest yellow, placing them in a bag as if they were pieces of gold and not bits of candy that rot and stick to the inside of children's pockets.

He counts bottles of black beer the way a *gabbai* might count Torah crowns. He may even make a ritual of drawing breath. And when it is Saturday afternoon, after morning prayers, and he returns from Synagogue to eat a bowl of *cholent* with a bit of *challah* and *schmaltz*, he rises from the table slowly, the long parts of him appearing from somewhere beneath the tabletop, gaining height like a building being topped by one story after another until he stands in his new high leather boots, his hands on his belly, and turns to lie down in the front room, boots half on and half off the sofa cushion, to let the weight of the meal settle itself.

Everything in the room waits around him. His patient attendants sense a disturbance and wait for the master to be right again, to give off the proper smell and sounds. The old lamps wheeze, the oilcloth on the floor offers up a sigh, the curtain rods hang a little heavier, the *mezuzot* on their inward slant stand erect with tension and the big black stove in the kitchen puffs smoke, dusts the rooms with silt, swings its heavy portals until Reb Menachem gives a climactic late afternoon burp, sighs and puts his high leather boots back on the floor.

But the house's Sabbath calm is still a day off, and now the kitchen is a bustle of chopping and boiling and pickling, and Reb Menachem Mendel must make his way to his leasehold and be back in time for evening prayers. But he doubts his speed, and he wonders if the way is passable, and he even considers the wear on his new boots. So, he hesitates.

He thinks of the shortcut he must take—beside Plock Street and the tar pit—alongside the fields and fruit trees of the District Authority where in summer there are masses of field flowers, gardens of reseda and cress, pools of asters and dahlias, elaborate rows of rose bushes and oleander, tobacco blossoms and sunflowers as high as your head. In summer the nearby brook pushes a mountain of blossoms, blown and dumped there by the keepers of the gardens, toward the forest in the west. All this beauty is silent gentile beauty, a place where Jews rarely go, a place whose pungent fragrance is sweet and incomprehensibly good. But it is strange, still.

The District Authority's house is surrounded by these gardens. It stands directly across the brook from where Reb Menachem and his fellow Jews gather to perform *Tashlich* on Rosh Hashanah. As the community turns out its pockets and sends its sins away with the current, they also look across at the District Authority's house, which looks to them like an empty husk, the abandoned hideout of a mysterious cabal.

In the winter the grounds surrounding the District Authority's house are buried. The fruit trees bend under the weight of snow, and each sharply pruned rose bush shows four or five fingers to the sky.

Reb Menachem curses his father as he opens the front door of his house, curses and then retracts the curse, wishing his father had not bought the lease on a piece of land so close to the District Authority's house. It is an inappropriate place for a Jew to have an interest. But he reminds himself that this bit of land is the only object of real value his father left him.

Menachem Mendel makes his way along Plock Street holding the collar of his coat up around his chin, not against the cold because it has been a brilliant mild blue day in winter, the sky like a block of pale marble, high and swirling, the breeze soft and fresh. Bits of mud show alongside the fieldstones where the snowdrifts are melting.

Menachem Mendel puts his collar up against the town to become more self-effacing, even less visible, so that no one will ask him where he is going before the Sabbath. His answer to this, he is sure, is guaranteed to elicit a clucking and braying from passersby: "Oh, Reb Menachem, it's so far, and such a goyish place to go just before Sabbath." To this he would answer, "Not so far. Not so far. I have to go to hand over the deed to the man who has bought my leasehold from me. And I must do it today because the money from the sale must be in hand by Monday. Or I wouldn't be doing this before the Sabbath."

But no one calls out to him. And soon he has left the street for the shortcut by the white-blanketed trees and the snow-filled pools of flattened asters trapped under the season's first snow, which came and never went. The trees are humpbacked under their burden, humpbacked white men against the afternoon sky, which darkens now toward the early winter dusk. Reb Menachem walks alongside the brook, which is not frozen but does not appear to move. It is a flat silver pan holding up snow-covered tangles of root, rigid frozen rushes, soft pillows of snow. These things transform themselves in the darkening light into other things. For a moment a beaver, then the back of a bear and the nose of a seal are visible in the still water.

Reb Menachem begins to regret setting out, or at least his lateness in setting out, for it was impossible for him to postpone the trip beyond this afternoon. The money he will receive in exchange for the title to the lease is to be exchanged for lawyer's fees and the other charges accrued when on the first of the new week his daughter, with her son, go to Warsaw to pick up the passports that await them in an office on Krochmalna Street. Reb Menachem knows Krochmalna Street because he traveled once to Warsaw to see a play presented by a Yiddish theater troupe, and the kosher restaurant at which he and his wife ate dinner was on the same street. His wife still talks about the uniforms worn by the waitresses, black and white with little aprons over the skirts. The uniforms made a greater impression on her than the play itself. An even greater impression than the blintzes they ate and than Warsaw in its late summer haze.

His daughter would go to the office on Krochmalna Street, pay for her visas and whatever else the authorities there could imagine had to be paid for, and then she and her son would continue to Gdynia to board a ship bound for Canada. All this is beyond Reb Menachem, and he slows his pace as he thinks of the streets in Warsaw with their massive curbstones and the electric trams piling up at intersections, the laundry hanging out the windows of gray apartment blocks.

His boots settle deeper into the snow. The brook, barely audible beside him, begins to vanish in the early dusk, its silver face blending with the shimmering wind-blown snowdrift. Reb Menachem tries to picture all the imponderables of his daughter's journey. He wonders why her husband was so intent on leaving Poland to begin with. How he could have left a child and a young wife behind, offering his family nothing but the promise that he would send for them. What would the immigration people in Warsaw say about these mysterious Canadian visas, arranged for at a time when Canada's borders had long been closed to foreigners? He fears for what the ship will bring. He has heard stories of filthy holds and dangerous profiteers who kidnap children—and of course the food, the food. How could his daughter eat it? And then his befuddlement over all this carries over to his musings about Canada—The Unknown—where there would be no kosher food or any community fit for his children. Only prairie and cattle and rimrock.

The path alongside the brook becomes rougher, thinner, with more branches and stumps in the way. Reb Menachem steps over the bits of wood and brush when he can, trying to avoid the clumps of snow piled on them. When his foot lands on one and then releases it, the branch cracks like a whip at his heels, glancing off the backs of his knees, sending snow in a spray up his back. The countryside conjures up its own swells and peaks. It is an ocean of snow that teases him, threatens to swallow him up.

He fears more and more that he will have to turn back, his business incomplete, if he is to be on time for evening prayers. He hesitates. He thinks, or tries to think, of Canada, watches his boots sink into the snow and brush so that he does not see the District Authority's house until he has almost tripped over its stairs and fallen by its broad wooden door.

Reb Menachem puts his hands up against the shingled side of the house as if he must ward it off, a beast let out of its cage. He closes his eyes, leans against the outer wall to straighten himself and regain his balance while his heart races and the blood pounds in his neck and in his head.

The District Authority's house takes up the whole landscape. It fills the sky and hangs out in a lazy arch over the brook. It is hideous with its broken thatch roof and its blackened windows, its tin chimney pot that peeks like a crooked turret out of its eaves.

It is the strangeness of the house, a whole life of looking at it from a distance and wondering what came and went in it, which plans and decrees were prepared there, that makes the old shack fearsome to Reb Menachem with his boots fixed in the snow beside it in the late afternoon calm.

He can barely believe, does not believe, that this house is just an administrative office and not a den of witches and devils. It sits in the fine gentile silence, beside the gray brook, blotting out the sky and the land and the water. He turns to escape it. Its tin pot turret and its shabby shingles. Its peeling-paint door, three planks held together by a fourth nailed crosswise over them.

But something holds him. His boot catches. His foot will come out of the boot if he pulls hard enough. He will leave the left boot, covet the right, make a wool-stockinged lunge through the drifts and abort his effort to barter his leasehold such a short time before the Sabbath. But something holds on to him, is pulling, trying to drag him back up the stairs of the District Authority's house to greet whatever waits behind the shuttered windows. Reb Menachem fights. He pulls at his foot, drags it out of the drift hiding the thing that has taken hold of him. And suddenly the brook is very loud—gurgling and laughing—and all the bits of brush covered in snow are snapping up out of their hiding places like snakes rising from their lairs, and the snow flies around him in a swirl, the little beaver's white nose pokes up out of the silver brook, and Reb Menachem is not sure if he has one or two of his high leather boots on, if his left foot is numb with cold or still warm and dry. The edge of the forest on the far side of the brook dances for him—up close and then very far away—like a band of calligraphy on a gray screen that has been put there for him to read. He sees black and gray lines and points as incomprehensible as his incomplete vision of the Canadian steppe.

Down the path between the District Authority's buried asters and dahlias he runs. He runs by the snow-bent trees in their neat lines, along a well-traveled path to the edge of Plock Street where he pauses, takes a breath and then hits the pavement of fieldstones in midstride and races up it, both of his long legs and one arm swinging, the other hand on his hat to hold it down. The passers-by who see him stop to watch Reb Menachem lope through the market toward his home, and each, to a person, thinks, "Such a pious man, Reb Menachem. Never late for Sabbath prayers."

Max's grandmother's line rings and rings.

"She must be out for a walk."

The phone rings the moment Max puts the receiver down. It cannot be his grandmother because she doesn't know Sara exists, but Max picks up the phone fully expecting to hear his grandmother say, Max you could at least tell me when you won't be at home. I need you to buy me a quart of milk and an egg loaf, sliced.

It's Ruth on the other end of the line.

"Let me talk to Sara."

Max hands the phone to Sara, who lifts her head off her fist and puts the phone between the two. Her features settle into a frown and then loosen into a smile. She catches Max's eye as she listens. There is a long pause during which Sara says nothing. She pulls at an eyelash.

"I'd believe it."

Another pause.

"He wanted to take you for Chinese food at two o'clock in the morning? I hope you drove him home."

Sara pulls at Max's arm and points at him, mouthing, "YOUR FATHER."

"Well, you shouldn't have let him drive. He always says that, that he'll sleep in the car."

"What is it?" Max takes the cord in both hands and pulls. Sara covers the receiver with her palm.

"It's all right, Max. He's all right."

Ruth's voice, almost a shout, can be heard ten feet from the receiver.

"He took you on a tour of the funeral home. Jesus, Ruth. You could've taken a rain check."

The room is suddenly very hot, the heat of the early afternoon leaking through the pinpricks in the burlap blind.

"The man is incorrigible. He has nothing to do except count his money and pester Max to learn the business. I know he means well, but he always seems to take the wrong route to the right end."

There are flowers in a vase on the high-legged table by the window. In the heat their smell is broad and corrupt, like rotting fruit. The blooms have gone dry and are dying, husks sprinkling the floor, skittering in the shade. They make the same sound as the caragana bushes behind Max's father's apartment, which pop like a rhythm section throughout the late summer.

Sara smiles up at him from the bed as he pulls on his pants, wavering a little on one foot, his socks popping out the ends of his pant legs where he left them the night before. She is laughing with Ruth, laughing at his father, and at the whole laughable life of a widowed undertaker who sleeps in his car.

Max puts his T-shirt on inside out and then turns it round to get it right.

"I'm going to find out what's up with my grandmother," he shouts, barely interrupting Sara's laughter. "I'm going to find her and find out if she needs an egg loaf."

"What?"

But she says this to his back as he opens the door to escape the hot room and the rhythm of dying flowers.

On the front step he realizes he has left his belt hanging on a chair. He considers going back for it, not quite himself with his waist unadorned.

The sun barrels down, a heavy silent storm. The grass whistles in its lazy length. Bees travel boldly up and down the rusty drain-pipes sounding a mad percussion that is carried away on the breeze.

A great white Cadillac fills the road and chuckles by in the heat. Max follows, reading the car's brightening and dimming rear lights as unavoidable signals that direct him not to his grandmoth-er's but to the Café des Westens.

Once Max has gone, Sara shuts the book and pulls her shoes from under the bed. She takes a pair of dark glasses from the pocket of a jacket that hangs over a chair. The report for the Tattooist League is stacked neatly, copied in triplicate. She slips the pages into a manila envelope. The cat follows her to the door where she must use a foot to keep him inside the apartment as she pulls the door shut.

Sara carries her package under one arm, the other hand free to pull at the leaves of trees she passes, to trail along the tips of fence pickets, to set her hair behind one ear. The intersections are deserted, the parking lots in front of taco stands are empty and a train clatters west over the Fourth Street overpass. Empty cattle cars, red sport convertibles tipped nose to nose, the rusted funnels full of Saskatchewan potash. She thinks of Max the way a mother thinks of her child, with tenderness, sadness, a touch of fear. The afternoon air is warm and still, and at the pollster's offices she opens the broad glass door to a blast from the over-cooled lobby, the sepulchral breeze of air-conditioning on high. At the security desk, a guard who recognizes her smiles and waves. He looks silly in his guard's cap, with fake epaulets on his shoulder—a bit like a child in party costume—and he is still smiling as the elevator opens to let her in.

Street Fights & Unexpected Visits

Ostrovsky and Martin sit in the empty café in a booth by the window where they can watch the people in the street and feel the sun on their necks. The light leaps past them in yellow bars, spots of dust caught glimmering on the way to rest on the red and black linoleum squares. Nothing stirs but the two men's backsides, their big arms sweeping the tabletop, their heads turning quickly when a woman passes on the sidewalk outside.

Ostrovsky and Martin are like meters installed to measure everything that passes on the sidewalk. The counting they do has no outcome, provides no tabulated results. They count and qualify people and cars and the weather out of instinct, burying what they learn as if it comprises unspeakable primordial information. They beat down the day, its long slow waste, its silence within the café, the chairs and glasses and the silver-topped counter reduced to a petrified state. The room is as pure as a stand of virgin forest, light twinkling, bare spots sparkling, clearings unexplored, the high pale ceiling as unmarked as a cloudless sky. Together, Ostrovsky and

Martin, explorers with no real treasure in mind, break ground.

"I sat with them yesterday."

"So you sat with them yesterday."

"So I have things to tell you."

"What things?"

"Things they say. Things they do."

"That's gossip, Martin."

"News, not gossip."

"What about your old grandfather, Martin. His fear of *lashon hora,* of evil words spoken bringing the speaker bad luck."

"My grandfather is dead, Ostrovsky. Dead and historic."

"But still very dear to you. And gossip never pleased him, Martin."

"This isn't gossip. It's news. News about people. There's nothing more interesting than news about people."

"So?"

"You want to know what they talk about?"

"No."

"Why not?"

"It's none of our business. They're young. We're not a part of their world."

"Like hell we're not. They're friends of my kid, Ostrovsky. Because you have no children you can play the objective observer."

"It's just a matter of decency."

"Decency? If my son's wasting his life it's a matter of decency?"

"He's not wasting his life, Martin. You're wasting my time and this day screaming about it."

"Screaming? I'm not screaming!"

"You're screaming, Martin."

"So I'm screaming, but this is no small concern."

"Then tell me. Tell me your big discovery."

"Oh, very detached you are. Server of drinks and omelettes. Big owner of a trendy place where bums and bums-to-be hang out. You get interviewed for some upscale magazine, and you think you've arrived. Just remember, Ostrovsky, your father was a loud-mouthed butcher who tattooed Cossacks for money between long shits in the woods."

"What is this now, Martin? Are you going to tell me something or just yell your head off?"

"Tell you something."

"Good. Tell."

The sunlight falls between them, and the cars motor by in pairs like friends, drivers watching each other."

"I'll tell you what they talk about."

"There's so much to tell you already forgot?"

"Just settle down, Ostrovsky. I'm thinking."

"Thinking of nothing."

"Thinking."

"You really take it out of me, Martin. That I have to sit here on such a nice day—just look at the sun—and listen to you carry on."

"Buildings."

"They talk about buildings."

"Yes."

"Horrifying."

"And cars."

"Oh God. Not cars."

"Also cigar bands and matchboxes and music."

"I think you should have them arrested."

"But it's the way they talk about these things. As if everything's trivial. They dismiss everything. Life is a joke. And the things they get caught up in! Spinning out stupid anecdotes and innuendo."

"You distilled this philosophy from one evening's conversation."

"You think that's too hasty."

"No, Martin, I think it's very astute."

"You're making fun of me, Ostrovsky."

"That is an accusation I would always deny coming from you."

"But the years are flying by, Ostrovsky. The summer is gone.

They're not kids anymore, and they continue to reject the world. Year after year they become more and more removed. Outside everything. And cynical. You should hear them talk."

"What do *we* talk about, Martin?"

"What do you mean, what do *we* talk about?"

"I mean what are we clearing up this afternoon? We talk about buildings and cars and music and we gossip."

"Not so, Ostrovsky. That's not so."

"Uh huh."

"We talk about other things."

"Such as?"

"Our parents."

"Mere familiar gossip."

"You're saying that to make me mad."

"You tell me about your grandfather, I tell you about mine. We tell each other the same stories over and over, changing them from week to week to make things more interesting."

"Which stories do you change?"

"I can't tell you that."

"Why not?"

"It would ruin all the surprise."

"And which stories do I change?"

"Most every one you know."

"Name one I've changed."

"You're tempting me, Martin. We're going to tread into dangerous waters here."

"Just name one I've changed and quit pontificating."

"Oh, touché. All right, you may not be aware of this, but your grand centerpiece, that story you're always telling about your grandfather and the Cossack, you reinvent that one every time you tell it."

"Now, of all the things to smear, Ostrovsky. Couldn't you pick something else to make fun of?"

"Yes, I could, but I've kept notes on that one."

"Notes?"

"Mental notes. It would be a shame to lose some of your favorite versions. There may be a use for them some day. For now they're just the thing to shut you up when you tell me your kid does nothing but waste valuable time. You have your own obsessions, Martin. And that Cossack story is unmatched among them, I'd say. Now I give you a certain amount of leeway on this one because you were never in your grandfather's house on Plock Street, so you're bound to be reconstructing, rearranging. But, to begin. The old mother is most often at a table, prayer book open before her, one hand over her eyes. It's evening, probably Sabbath. She has very white hair tied in a tight bun. A young woman, not very interested in what is being done, sits beside her. The young woman throws a shadow. The older woman, presumably, is too thin and transparent to throw shadows. How am I doing so far?"

"That's how I see it."

"Yes, but the variations are marvelous. In one version the old mother disappears but for a spot of red fabric and the white-fringed collar on her dress. And the sullen young woman, no longer seated, is bent over the table backward, her red stockings rolled down at the knee, her shoes tangled up in the tattered rug. And the bits of the room come and go just as the people in it do. How do you see it, Martin?"

"Why should I tell you anything, so you can mock my impression of it?"

"Because you want to tell me. . . . Tell."

"Not if you're going to make fun of it all."

"I won't make fun of you, Martin."

The two men become quiet. A woman passes on the sidewalk in the sun, a shopping bag knocking against her leg with each step. A wind is up, pushing her hair into her face.

"What gives you the right to test my memory, Ostrovsky?"

Ostrovsky settles his chin into open palms. Martin cannot resist the temptation to retell the tale.

"A very brown room it was, I've been told. With fancy molding where the wall met the ceiling. And the door that led out to the front hall was green. The color matched the chair backs and seats, as well as the seat of a sofa where my grandfather used to lie in the afternoon. The ceiling was blue. A bluish gray made light and dark by the lamps scattered around the room. All chintz-shaded, like the lights that burn late in a Gypsy fortune teller's caravan. There was a long-leafed plant up high on a shelf. It crowned the head of anyone who sat beneath it, like a canopy. There were very few paintings on the wall, graven images being out of favor in all but the most secular homes. There was a gray carpet on the floor that was always bunching up and getting tangled around table legs. A child underfoot, reading a book with legs spread, toys in the corners. A kite. A punchinella. A gold horn full of dust. Shutters on the windows. An interminable silence settled over the place."

"But you've described it differently, Martin. In broader terms, a less exact layout, shall we say. A view from outside, with windows unshuttered, heads moving around in the lighted squares. A cat arching its back on the sill. A very orange slice of moon sitting on the rooftops."

"Big orange slice of moon! Now who does that sound like, Ostrovsky, you or me? I'd say you, for some ridiculous reason, have. . . ."

Ostrovsky stops him with an open hand held between them.

"We come in very fast through the window, Martin, and we see no toys, no molding up high by the blue ceiling. We sweep in along the floor like a bat, skitter over the dusty wood past a woman's shoe, around a chair leg. We navigate the nap of the rug until we land on a bare ankle, a long leg dangling beneath a table, toes wiggling. And the shadows have taken over, Martin. The shadows have turned the room into a death room. And everyone is dressed for winter, in overcoats and fur collars, shrouds sweeping down around the legs of children who gather in corners to keep warm. And we circle, alighting on the shoe, the dangling leg,

the shoe, the bare ankle, the shoe, until the whole room it seems
—and everyone in it—can be stood in the shadows between that
ankle and that shoe."

Ostrovsky lets his hands hover above the table as if he is performing a trick.

"I have no idea what you're talking about."

"I just record these things, Martin. And there is some question
as to how many times the Cossack hetman banged on the door.
Also a question of how hard he banged. A candle may have fallen
over, but this is an inconsistent detail. The flames may only have
flickered once, in warning, long shadows playing on the walls.
And it is unclear who answered the knock at the door. One version has it that it was your grandfather, Reb Menachem, but it
seems more likely that it was the daughter of one of his sisters who
opened the door, the girl being a good deal more courageous
than her over-learned uncle. And who knows if it would have been
different if the old man had answered the knock. Possibly then the
hoodlums would have only taken the old man's boots, a few
pieces of silverware, a cheap horn that the children had left in the
hall. The strangers at the door might only have pressed their fingers into Reb Menachem's ribs so that he, all six feet of him, col-
lapsed in the hall with his fine new leather boots sitting heels up
on the threshold for the hetman to admire. Reb Menachem would
have lost only his nerve and a bit of pride. Instead, the little girl
went out the door as quickly as if she'd taken flight. The blue hem
of her skirt, the tips of her heels, the suddenly visible pink underside, vanished. As lost to all as youth itself. And only then, over
the unconscious Reb Menachem, who fainted in the excitement,
over the six foot length of him, stepped all his family to see only
horses' tails as the Cossacks rode off. The big brown muscular
haunches. Flying saddlebags. And one small blue package being
held to the side of a horse by a long arm under a very strange
orange slice of moon."

Ostrovsky looks out the window as if the moon might be hung

there in honor of the tale. He raises two fingers to his forehead and rubs his brow.

"One might even think of the rider performing tricks with his cargo, getting half off his horse and stretching one arm out along the ground. The other hand and a leg holding tightly on to the saddle."

Certainly Martin could see this. He saw the ground rushing by the little girl's face so clearly that he felt sick. He heard the rider's loose shirt flapping in the wind, sensed the horse's dumb driven need to break across the square. The family left behind to stare. Imps and ghouls. Their eyes widening—as big as saucers—staring after the big-assed horses. Nothing to say, the women running out ahead, the men behind in defeat. A streetlight above the street, another bright face without features, its perfect profile belittling the uneven moon, which is blurred by wisps of reddened cloud floating beside it.

The town in its night colors—the deep blue trees, the purple roadways, the soft yellow stone buildings, the violet grass sparkling in the dark like a bed of gems.

Certainly Martin could see this.

And what it is Ostrovsky has made up Martin is no longer sure. And what it is he has told Ostrovsky himself he can no longer remember. And what is memory and what is pure creation is unclear. But he feels certain he has not made up the vision of the little blue dress being carried over uneven fieldstones.

Ostrovsky smiles at him.

There is the sound of boot heels in the entranceway. Martin and Ostrovsky turn.

"What d'ya say boys?"

A very tall policeman stands with his hands in his pockets just inside the door. His head nearly touches the lamp that hangs from the ceiling.

The cop moves stiffly in his ironed-and-starched shirt and pants. He has his collar buttoned up very high, and there is an innumerable arrangement of buckles and flaps and buttons—snaps as well—that keep him covered up, neatly uniformed. His legs, like big bridge ponts, take him across the room, feet falling on cracks in linoleum, breaking his mother's back over and over as he goes. At the counter he puts his elbows down carefully in two well-worn spots and rests his chin on open palms.

"Ostrovsky?"

The proprietor answers his customer's call, falling into position behind the counter.

"The usual?"

"The regular."

"It's a little hot out for hot chocolate, isn't it, Sergeant?"

"Hot drinks cool you off when it's hot. The guy who sold me my insurance policy told me that. He must know."

Ostrovsky presents a mug—turns the handle a shade to the left so it is easily grasped—and a packet of hot chocolate mix. He plugs in the kettle.

"Got a new kind of drink, eh?"

The Sergeant reads the label on the hot chocolate packet.

"Twice as much in it, but it's the same price as the old one."

"Twice as much in it, eh?"

"Just put half in your cup, and I'll save the other half for you."

"But what'll I do with the other half?"

"Well, I'll save it for you, and you can have it next time you're in."

"But it still costs the same?"

"Same for you, Sergeant."

The cop looks up from the packet at Ostrovsky.

"So I can get two cups out of this?"

"I think that's the best bet."

"So how about you saving the other half, and I'll have another cup later."

Ostrovsky pours the boiling water into the mug and takes the half-emptied packet out of the policeman's hand.

"Sounds like a good idea."

The Sergeant drinks in tiny careful sips. His throat makes a clicking noise each time he swallows. The steam rising from the cup makes his face shine with sweat.

"I came by to warn you. There's going to be a lot of action out front in a bit. We're routing a demonstration off Eighth Avenue. It's disturbing all the shoppers and slowing up the LRT. A real pack of idiots and photographers will be passing by your place. I'm telling everyone along this street in case you want to close for the afternoon."

"Who's demonstrating?" Martin and Ostrovsky ask in unison.

"Anarchists. They're having a convention. They're not really a club I'm familiar with. If you took a quick look at the bunch of them you might think it was 1968 again. There's a lot of khaki and cutoffs and ponytails on the guys. Some women are running around with their shirts off, mostly the big-breasted ones, I noticed. Might not be your kind of customer, Ostrovsky."

"Thanks Sergeant, but I think I can deal with the excitement without closing up the café."

"I would call it unwise to serve these characters. I wouldn't think that would do any good for the reputation of this establishment."

Martin puts his nose against the glass, turns his neck so he can see up the street, westward.

"Nothing out there just now."

"Wait half an hour or so."

The Sergeant puts the mug down on the countertop and licks his lips. He crosses the café and stands by the door, wiping his boots on the mat, as if he has wandered into a field of something he can't quite recognize.

"You'll have something to watch soon enough."

Martin has his hands on the window now, bracing his weight as he puts one knee up on a bench in a booth. He stares up the street.

"Nothing out there, Ostrovsky."

Ostrovsky disappears through the swinging doors that hide the kitchen. There is stock to take. Cans to straighten up and sticky pine shelves to rinse clean. A boarded-up hole in the wall must be properly covered before the fire inspector makes a surprise visit and starts making threats. There is the music of griddles on burners, the scraping down of cutting boards. The awning over the restaurant's back window sings its rough tune as Ostrovsky puts the S-shaped crank in the proper joint and turns, winding the red and white covering out over the window to prepare for the late afternoon sun, which heats up the back of the café and makes it impossible to work.

Martin is at the front window, moving from booth to booth, trying to decide which vantage point offers the best view of the street.

"Ostrovsky!"

There is no answer.

"Ostrovsky! I think I'll take a walk and try to see what's coming. Ostrovsky?"

The awning gives its final whine.

"What?"

"I'm going to see who's marching."

"Tell me if you see your son, Martin."

"Very funny. I'll tell you if I see any ladies. Oh. I forgot. There's one other thing."

Martin yells over the counter through the closed kitchen doors.

"I picked up something one of them wrote on a napkin last night. I'll leave it by the cash."

"Fine Martin. Go look for your son."

Martin puts the folded paper under the wind-up barkeep's feet. He leaves the café but stops by the window outside to watch as Ostrovsky comes through the swinging doors, pushing a cart piled high with his trademark drinking glasses, some plastic, some glass, some gifts at gas stations. He stops by the counter and lifts the toy's feet off the paper. Martin leaves him reading by the pile of glasses. With one eye slightly squinted to focus, Ostrovsky says to the room:

> Let me see these
> Fancy tales of smoke.
> The ships of Diego Velazquez
> skirting the long
> coast at daybreak,
> breaking water,
> wild hopes
> and greed
> rushing in the
> heads of his sailors
> like
> wind.
>
> These fancy tales,
> of missed opportunities
> with the money changer's
> daughter,
> her bell sleeves and skirt
> decorating street corners
> in the afternoon haze,
> as the Official Parade
> travels down the
> thoroughfare,
> the fat horses
> leaving such a barrage
> of shit
> that an entire
> army of men is employed
> with scoops and brooms
> to make the mess disappear.

Oh fancy tales.
these are someone's
nightdreams.

The pink-painted house
at evening,
the squall of cats
running everywhere,
scattering like roaches
at the arrival of
visitors.
The books in lines,
the desk made of elm wood
(who cares what wood
the desk was made of?)
the chair where the
writer/man/and icon
himself
may have written
ten or twelve
sentences once
on an afternoon
between absinthe
and cigars
and hot dogs, his square white beard
like the markings on a ship's sail
turning the corner 'round the peninsula
at daybreak.
These fancy tales of smoke.
Put 'em in your pipe and smoke 'em.

I can only tell you,
or promise
and say to you as

unequivocally
as I ever have,
that there is pleasure
in them,

Fancy tales of smoke.

The bride is filled up
with her happiness.
She is white, ivory,
diamond,
satin,
brown-eyed and more
beautiful than fear.
She will never come back
from this visit
to her greatest dream.
She draws ribbons
down from the sky,
the children trail
behind her,
the men break off everything
before her
and bend at the waist.
She is in the one place
she has always hoped to be.

The groom can
be found
in his well-known
chiaroscuro gloom.
He is obscured
by all the moorish
shade,

caught and flailing
in Velazquez's sails,
robbed of the treasure
found once when the
ships
rounded
the peninsula at
daybreak.
And he brings into his
heart
all the happiness
and beauty of his soon
to be
wife.
But to waste it.
In his wedding robes,
his finery,
his grace,
he forgets the woman, his bride,
even hates her for her happiness
and thinks only
of
fancy tales of smoke.

Father

I find father, his pant legs flapping like flags in the wind. His eyes disappear beneath his brow as we collide in the alcove of the café. He shrinks at first, surprised and defensive, but then stretches to his full height above me, his forehead as high as the eaves, his eyes, deep-set and huge, are worlds I am reflected in. His hair moves in the warm afternoon wind, in need of a comb. He rises out of the sidewalk, a permanent fixture. He attracts all the light and sound and memory in the town to the very street corner where we stand. And the heat seems to come to us, to hang above us and linger at our feet. The wind that was once everywhere now blows only for us, for him really, and I am by chance in the eye of his hurricane.

The season breaks over us and pours its sad end down the faces of the buildings, rains over the rooftops, hails down into the gutters, the brief hot summer in its last shade shedding its coat in the blink of an eye. A heartbreak takes its place: the not-yet-autumn, no-longer-summer of the late afternoon. And we stand in it, father and I, like two wanderers who have come to the same part of a strange town at the exact moment to ask each other the same question.

Father takes his hand out of his pocket and wipes his brow. There is color in his cheeks. He turns toward the street to watch the crowd pressing up it.

My voice comes out of my throat no louder than the scuff of a shoe on the pavement, saying, "You took them there to shame me and to shame yourself, in the middle of the night, drunk, and now they've told their friends and their families, and you have become some kind of ghoul in the lore of your town so that I feel ashamed for you and I want to hide from you. . . ."

But my spoken words have no identity. They are objects disguised, garbled code, and I am like a machine overheating in the sun, chucking parts all over the road.

Father offers an explanation. He does not address me. He addresses the heat, which is listening far more closely than I. He addresses the street, which is splattered with the last of the summer, dressed down now in its heartbreak. The crowd comes up it in a crazy rush, arms, legs, camera lenses pointing this way and that, bare-breasted women taunting the whirring shutters, taunting any man who will look, shaking fingers that announce, *There! You looked!* And the mounted police take up the rear, their horses dropping huge green piles all over the street, but the big brutes are jittery, spooked by the crowd.

The police are not controlling things. They send everything that much more out of control by bringing their big braying machines into the fray. The young people see that the mounted men and women who came to scare them are really there to be abused, and there is a great waving of arms and poking of fingers before the horrified horses. The odd luckless demonstrator takes a long slide through the mounds of shit left by the nervous beasts and goes home caked like a farmer's fence post. Red Emma Goldman goes up and down on placards, as does a profile of Trotsky gazing through pince-nez. He stares at Luxemburgs,

Liebknechts, Kropotkins. Bakunin wears a hat. Slogans flash in the haze, patches on the knees of jeans, bumper stickers stuck on bums, signs all saying the same things about freedom, bread, internationalism, struggle. Exclamation points are everywhere.

One car, honking, prowling stubbornly behind the crowd, tries to force a way through the action.

Father and I watch the melee pass the café. First the slipping and braying crowd, then the stubborn gold Impala, the driver, his shock of white hair straight up on top of his head, hands tight on the wheel, wearing the stubborn expression of an old ideologue, eyes barely above the dash, refusing to stray from the slow and useless path he's chosen.

In all the excitement I forget my long list of resentments and the angry speech I planned to make.

A couple detaches themselves from the stragglers circling in the middle of the street, and disappear, arm in arm, into the café. The street shivers, shaking off the excitement of the just cause, and becomes its flat purposeless self. A garbage can lid rolls in the gutter. One of the Impala's hubcaps hovers by on the wind.

"I'm on my way over to your grandmother's, if you feel like joining me."

"Is it her day for shopping?"

"No. Someone else is coming to shop. Those brothers from Sweden who want to buy the house are sending their agents."

"I thought that pair had finally given up on her."

"Seems it's become a point of honor with them. Her corner is the key to their plans. And she humors them to find out what her lot's worth this week."

Father waves at Ostrovsky, who stands behind the glass door of the café and smiles, his hands pressed on his belly, his face catching the sun that sneaks under the awning. Ostrovsky looks past us at the marchers and the police left blocking the road. Most of the crowd has turned a corner, headed, it seems, for the fair grounds. There remain only a few mounted policemen and the braver hangers-on who taunt them. One particularly loud marcher is thrown down and held there under a boot heel.

"My father's the DA in this town," he yells up from his spot on the asphalt.

"There are no DAs in Canada, kid."

The policeman removes his riding gloves.

"Shut up or I'll squash you."

The lady from the house across the street has ventured away from her mantelpiece and stepped onto her lawn. She shouts at the remnants of the demonstration, as if it is one large personality, telling it to go home. To smarten up. To respect other people's privacy.

A girl comes rolling a hoop across the asphalt. The air stands still, silent, as eyes turn to watch her balancing act. A collective gaze follows her shadow up the street until she disappears behind a light pole.

Real Estate

Max joins his father, imagining himself as the protector of things old and fragile. Beyond the granite city hall and a couple of old cars, what was there in town more antique than his grandmother's house? Nothing had been passed on to him in the way of real mementoes. He had no Polish trinkets. What little had made the Atlantic crossing was buried in drawers, locked in safety deposit boxes. His father showed him things, then hid them away again. The affidavit dated 1921, by which a farmer named Peter Fokke promised the Alberta government he would hire the Binders to work on his farm, SE of Section 31, Township 25, Range 2, west of the third meridian. The delousing certificate signed by one O.O. Rimbolt, medical examiner on the S.S. France, the pride of the fleet of ships that ran, according to the certificate's masthead, on "the world's greatest highway." A couple of photographs of stern men in uniform, standing before a felt backdrop where an ersatz forest shimmered, deep in its sleep of snow.

The few customs Max had become familiar with were acted out

around his grandmother's house. For years he had lifted the orange Sunbeam mower into the trunk of his father's car—and driven, or when he was too young, was driven—through the back streets of the downtown to the old house. The neighborhood was already being picked apart when he was a kid, houses being replaced by little office buildings, lots left useless, full of gravel and cast-off bedsprings. The building next door to the house had been renovated, the coffee shop at streetside where folk singers had made their debut, green, off the train from Saskatoon, became a hangout for lawyers and tourists. There was always something sad about coming to tend an ancient lawn in a neighborhood that was slowly being effaced.

The mower barely fit through the gate in the picket fence. Max parked it on the walk, dragging the cord up the front stairs and into the dark living room, which was cool behind drawn curtains. He plugged the cord into the only three-pronged outlet in the place and fed it back out the front door, down the steps to his machine. Then he pushed the mower around in the weeds, past the pockmarked lily of the valley where a flattened child's ball hid, older than himself he was sure, lost there during some aborted game. A pillar of dust trailed him as he walked the mower into the backyard. The mixture of grass and weed smelled like ripe apples being mashed as he cut it.

Martin and Max decide to drive, even though Martin's mother's house is no more than fifteen blocks away from the café, so they set out to get Martin's car.

The city is very small. The buildings are half-finished, smudges against an undefined horizon. Max and Martin pass through walls, step over rooftops. Fourth Street is a pencil sketch, charcoal dust flying on the breeze. Young women walk into the haze and disappear. Boys push sticks under one side of a fence and triumphantly pull out swords on the other. Girls braid each other's hair and toss the twisted lines at the horizon.

Max and Martin pass tall apartment blocks, wooden houses and churches. Their heels click, and they trip on uneven sidewalk stones. First Martin leads and then Max. From the far side of the street they look like uneasy strangers trying to outwalk each other. Martin is quiet, possibly hurt and angry for being dressed down by Max over the night before, but more likely he feels guilty that they are late. He trusts his mother to take care of her own business—she is a cannier business person than he, having navigated tougher times. Still, he prefers to be present, a comfort nodding in a kitchen chair. And he does not feel completely at ease with the idea of his mother having to confront a pair of strange men. There has been trouble in the neighborhood lately. Hoodlums posing as paperboys. Developers with shady methods of expropriation.

In front of Martin's apartment building, the window washer's ropes whistle in the wind. The granite knows one sad low note. Out back the dandelion gatherer is at work.

Martin backs the big car out of the garage. The streets, traffic, trees disappear behind them. Autumn flashes its red and yellow smile as they cross town.

When they arrive at the house and climb out of the car, Max feels that it has become cooler, shadows spilling from porchways, and among the rows of fence posts children count and dive for cover in the undergrowth, the afternoon's last rebels.

Max's grandmother stands holding the screen door open, half inside the house, half out. Two men take turns shaking her hand, fiercely and at length, with a tense nod to punctuate their wagging elbows.

"That's them."

"Sven and Bjorn?"

"No. Their agents." Martin spots the basement man, who stands beside a little red car parked at the curb, resting his hand on the canvas roof and bending over to admire the interior.

"It's a beauty," he yells across the yard. "Rambler American. Had one like it in '66 when I was working as a switchman in

Vancouver with the CPR. I'll tell you, the boys were jealous. Most of 'em rode CCMs in those days, if you know what I mean, like I do now. But I was a prize, cruising home down Melville Street."

Martin has a soft spot for the basement man, and he walks over to admire the car alongside him. As they talk, the basement man edges out into the street and away from the car. The Rambler is a kind of time machine, as red, its chrome as bright, as the day it rolled off the line.

Martin stands by the passenger side patting the front fender. "It's a beauty." He is alone now, ankle deep in the grass that has overgrown the paving stones.

The two agents come down the stairs of the house. One is dressed like a Hollywood gigolo, with a bolo tie hung loosely around his neck, a light brown suede vest over a navy shirt, which is buttoned at the cuffs and the collar. The gigolo's partner looks like a cross between a hairdresser and a soap opera star—he is taller and better coiffed, with the kind of black curls that are worn high, like a helmet. Both men have deep tans. Their skin is the color of expensive leather.

Max assumes that the two of them arrived early on purpose.

"Hi, son." The man with the bolo tie extends a tanned hand. With his other hand in his pocket, he touches, Max imagines, the button that ignites his smile, which is brilliant.

"Did you make her an offer she couldn't refuse?"

The bolo tie turns to his partner and laughs, then turns back to Max. "Your grandmother knows what she's doing, son. Don't you worry about her."

As Max watches them cross the street to their car, he notices the basement man, bent at the waist, creep from behind a bush beside their parked car. He straightens himself at the corner and makes a great show of checking both ways before he crosses the deserted intersection. He stops beside Max as the car starts, holding a knife with a curved blade that Max has seen his grandmother use to peel potatoes.

"I only flattened one," he whispers, slipping the knife into his pocket, and he disappears behind the house, whistling.

The car travels halfway down the block and stops in the middle of the road. The engine idles as the man with the bolo tie gets out to look at his shredded rubber. Max knows this is nothing more than the tiniest triumph, but it is a triumph all the same.

He follows his father up the neatly painted steps and stops on the landing. His grandmother watches the stalled car, wiping her hands on a dish towel.

"They come almost every day." She presents the latest installment in her card collection, which lists only a numbered company, and two names: JIM BROWN, SETH WHITE—REALTORS.

"Gotta be a joke." Martin hands the card back to his mother.

"It's no joke," she counters, citing the sum they have offered her, the terms of the deposit cheque they laid on the kitchen table, telling her to just tear it up if she wasn't interested, which she did, in front of them, slipping the shreds of twenty-five thousand dollars into her apron pocket.

Max feels a certain relief as he stands in the lowering light on the uppermost stair, but he realizes the future has come to his grandmother's house where for decades nothing has dwelt but the past. Since they have come this far, Max and Martin make an afternoon of it.

The House at Dusk

On the lawn the old basement man, seven years a tenant in the little room against the east wall, boiling beef, collecting things, his belly out, a cap on his head, bicycle pump between his thighs, takes the temperature of a piece of foam rubber with a plastic thermometer. Miss Duncan, the keeper of alley cats, is bent over in a lawn chair with her dearest one in her lap. The cat has no name. She calls the basement man the Thompson, as if he is something concrete and not a man. Max listens as they reminisce about a tenant who lived in the suite beside the basement man's, who smoked cigarettes in the backyard and peed in the corner most mornings at four A.M. He killed the grass to avoid flushing the toilet so the lady of the house wouldn't think he was rabble-rousing, though he did nothing with his time but go out for burgers, bring home his homework, take long drags in the backyard.

But still Mrs. Binder was suspicious. Why would someone have to pee at four in the morning?

Hunched over in their lawn chairs, they disagree over whether the boy was sick or just quiet.

"A sad quiet type." Miss Duncan rubs the cat's back.

"He was retarded." The basement man hasn't heard that these things are said euphemistically in an era more genteel than his. A logger and railman, he calls things as he sees them.

Miss Duncan doesn't care one way or another, since this has nothing to do with cats or the garden or herself.

And the light comes up, goes down, as clouds and the big trees interfere, the blue sky gone a little toward dusk, fading to purple at the edges. The horizon is the color of the inside of an iris at nightfall.

Up in the kitchen window, Martin takes dishes from the table to the sink. He is gray behind the glass. Max, down on the grass, watches the basement man pump a tire, check the valve for a leak with a thumbprint of spittle. Miss Duncan holds her orange and black prize against her flattened bosom, pulls a pin out of the little gray bun on top of her head and tickles her pet. All believers they are, the cat included, in the primacy of flower beds, of cluttered rooms, of dusk.

The shadows creep along the ground, the waver of laundry spooks the cat, and it leaps through the high grass behind a lilac bush. The basement man sits his foam on a chair and puts his weight against the back steps to show where they're rotten. The posts creak. He pushes a toe through lily of the valley. He knows he has Max's attention, so he talks without looking up.

"Your grandmother's been here a long time. I've been here seven years. She's the last one on the block. All the people who built this block are gone. The big man comes down here and buys everything up from under 'em."

"She's going to sell this house one day," Max says. "One day they'll offer more money than my grandmother can turn down, and then where's she going to go?"

"I don't know. I don't." The basement man checks his foam, this time with the palm of his hand. "Just the same. You better tell me where you're going to go."

Max has no answer. He tries to come up with something but words rattle in his head. A voice he cannot recognize, describing something he's forgotten. The words have nothing to do with the basement man and his question. He loses his train of thought as he tries to place the voice that said—her face is a gathering of shadows. A wonderful face. Full of storm clouds and darkening years.